Alone Y

Chapter 1
Written by
Shawn Downey

It was on the lower east of New York city a place where no one dare to go the, not so nice side of town, in a trailer park house number 5402 Willow Cres, Lisa Monroe gets ready for school, as she fumbles through her closet looking for something clean to wear, feeling frustrated she put on what she wore yesterday, that was pink t-shirt with gravy stains on it, and a pair of black jeans with holes in the knees, and worn out socks.

It all started when Lisa was starting school for the first time being picked. On because she is different, Lisa is a skinny girl with long brown hair and glasses kind of nerdy she doesn't care in fact that is the way she likes it she's not like any of the other girls, that are into makeup and dressing up in expensive clothes, she is in to video games getting dirty and loves fast paced action movies.

"Lisa you're going to be late for school again if you don't come out of your bedroom the school bus is here" shouted her mother,

Lisa ran out of her room headed out the door to the school bus past her stepfather Scott Hill. An out of work welfare case whose life's mission is to make everyone around him feel like crap.

Scott has been Lisa's stepfather since she started walking her real father left the picture when Lisa was first born, he too just like Scott didn't work and wasn't mature enough to raise a kid so, he packed his things and, left. Scott is a useless man who would, rather make Lisa's mother works three jobs to pay the bills and keep him drinking beer. Scott spends most of the time on his motorbike. He is a big man about six feet six and three hundreds plus pounds with long hair and tattoos on both arms. And yellow teeth with long hair that he wears in a ponytail.

Lisa got on to the bus went to the back of it sat in the back seats where she sits by herself on the bus because no one really bothers with her she pulls her head phones out of her back pack and puts music on she settles in for the ride to school.

Alone Volume 1

Lisa attends Junior high now and is in grade eight Lisa gets off the bus heads into the school where she dreads the day. As she is picked on day to day and no one does anything about it, Lisa went to her locker grabbed her books before the school bullies spot her Before they come to make her life miserable,

Lisa heads quickly to her class and takes her seat. The only one in the class, she waits for the bell to ring the kids to start coming in. Once the kids start coming they all stare at Lisa laughing and snickering to them-selves about how she was dressed this morning. Lisa had a dirty shirt on and ripped jeans and her hair uncombed.

Once all the kids were in their seats the teacher enters Lisa's teacher is nice to her. She seems to be the only one that is nice and will speak to Lisa. Mrs. Kay is her name she is one of the older teachers and has been teaching for a long time.

"Good morning class how is everyone today I hope you're ready to expand your minds and learn your lessons if you put away your books as promised yesterday we are having a test the class had surprised looks on their faces when Mrs. Kay said that she was going to give the test this morning. Don't be so surprised. I told everyone that there was going to be a test today but I didn't say what time this test will be worth half of your passing grade as we move on into the next term some of you will have different classes and some of you will be with me again" says Mrs. Kay.

Lisa got a lump in her throat she was scared she wasn't going to stay in Mrs. Kay's class anymore and that scared her.

"You can now open your exams and start you have all morning to finish it" instructs Mrs. Kay

The class opened the tests Lisa was the first one to get right down to working on the test she was sweating and anxious she didn't really study for this one so she is going to have to remember what she learned for this exam. The exam was long and intense covering everything that was taught for the term. Lisa was the first one done she check's her answers over to make sure that she was satisfied with her answers. She puts her pen down and closes the test. Turns it over and looks up, Mrs. Kay walks over to Lisa and grabs the test and looks at Lisa and says. "Are sure you have read the test right because you still have thirty minutes' left on the test?"

"Yes I am done Mrs. Kay. I was sure of myself. I think I did fine," says Lisa.

"Okay. I was just checking that's all. I have some concerns I think we need to get your mother in here, or your stepfather to have a talk. But I will talk to you more later on at lunch okay" says Mrs. Kay

Lisa sat back in her chair and hung her head she thought to herself about what Mrs. Kay had said. *I hope Mrs. Kay doesn't call Scott he doesn't really care about me and mom she is too busy working I thought I was doing so good I am not sure what concerns that she has*

The lunch bell rang and everyone headed out the door to the cafeteria for lunch except for Lisa, Mrs. Kay as promised wanted to see her for a minute at lunch. Mrs. Kay closes the door looks at Lisa.

"Have a seat dear" offers Mrs. Kay, Lisa looks at Mrs. Kay and says.

"I will stand thanks" says Lisa. Mrs. Kay leaned back in her chair and starts to talk

"Lisa my dear I have some concerns lately you have been coming to school with dirty clothes on hair uncombed and smelling like you haven't bathed in months, it is very worry some for me you're a very pretty girl, you need to start taking better care of yourself" explains Mrs. Kay. Lisa looks at Mrs. Kay with sad eyes she doesn't say much but Mrs. Kay can sense that she is unhappy.

"You're free to go now my dear have a good lunch" replies Mrs. Kay. Lisa heads out the door and to the court yard she doesn't have a lunch today so sits and reads a book and watches all the kids going in and out of the school looking at her like she is a stranger. Lisa doesn't let this bother. Her she ignores the people that are looking at her and making fun. Lisa reads until the lunch bell rang, she headed back to class and took her seat.

"Welcome back class," replies Mrs. Kay.

"I took a look at your exams I am happy with some of you but others I am not happy you can do better than that I know you can" replies Mrs. Kay , Mrs. Kay's eyes were staring at Lisa when she said this.

"The students that didn't do well I am going to give you a second chance to write the test again I have three names on my list that didn't do well at all and that really need to rewrite the exam the ones that have low marks it will be an option for you if you want to improve your mark" explains Mrs. Kay.

Mrs. Kay wrote the names on the board Lisa is one of them Lisa rolls her eyes as Mrs. Kay puts her name on the board if she could help it she was going to skip out on the detention that she is required to have with the teacher.

The day went on and Mrs. Kay taught her lessons. When the bell rang, everyone rushed out the door. The ones that had detention left to go to another room except for Lisa. She found a way to leave and get out of detention, when she is outside Lisa finally gets on the school bus to head home.

The school bus stopped in front of her house her stepdad Scott was sitting in his chair outside drinking beer and listening to his heavy metal music. He spots Lisa and turns down the music. He gets up out of his chair a little wobbly on his feet he stagers over to Lisa.

"Hey stupid how was school today did you get smarter or are you still stupid" insults Scott.

Lisa continued to walk away from Scott heads into the house to her room where she puts her backpack down heads to the kitchen for a snack, finding a bag of potato chips. She rushes to her room closes the door and sits on her bed to start doing homework. She heard Scott thumping around in the house, and then she saw the shadow of his feet at her door. Lisa jumped up off her bed and hid in the closet closing the door so that Scott wouldn't find her Scott came into Lisa's room and started to shout.

"I know you're in here you walked away from me that was rude. I was just asking you how school was and you walked away from me. Don't make me tell your mother she will give you a belt or maybe i will. You deserve it you, selfish brat," yells Scott.

Scott finally slammed the bedroom door heading back outside to finish his heavy metal music and his beer. Lisa heard the bike start-up She thought that this would be a good time to draw some attention to Scott. She heads to the living room window. Scott is leaving the trailer park. Lisa grabs the phone and calls the police on Scott for driving drunk.

"Police department," says the dispatcher

"Yes, I would like to report a crime in progress a fat man on a motor-bike driving drunk," reports Lisa.

The dispatcher took down the info then Lisa waited for the sound of the sirens to go off. It's New York; the cops are always after someone Lisa chuckled at what she did. She headed back to her room to read and lay on her bed to watch TV.

It was getting late and Lisa hadn't seen Scott since he left. Her mom should be coming home any minute now; Lisa decides to go cook some supper for her and her mom.

When her mom walks in she puts down her purse and walks to the kitchen.

"Hello sweetie supper smells good" replies Mom.

"Thanks I try" says Lisa

"So where is Scott at?" asks Mom.

"Last I seen him he was outside. When I got home from school he was sitting on his fat butt drinking beer and listening to his music. I heard the bike leave and he hasn't come back since" responds Lisa.

"That doesn't surprise me he is always out on the bike or drinking beer and listening to that god awful music he likes. I don't understand why he is the way that he is" says Mom.

"What do you see in him anyway? He doesn't work. You're working all the jobs, making all the money and he just sits and does nothing. It's not right mom, not at all," states Lisa.

"What was I supposed to do after your father ran off I worked hard to keep you in diapers and a roof over our heads. I needed a man to keep me happy and give me what I want in life. But I guess that is never going to happen" cries Mom.

Supper was cooked and Lisa and her mom sat at the table to eat together something they hadn't done for a while. The pair talked with mom asking Lisa how school has been going and why she doesn't bring friends around, during dinner the door-bell rang Mom got up to answer it when she finds there it was the police.

"Are you Mrs. Monroe?" asks the Officer

"Yes, I am her," answers Mrs. Monroe

"Do you know a Scott Hill, madam?" asks the Officer

"Yes, I do what happened?" asks Lisa's Mom.

"Mrs. Monroe, Mr. Hill was caught on his motorbike, six-times over the legal limit now when the dispatcher gave us the info we weren't told who called his licence had this address on it," replies the officer.

"I knew the day would come when he got caught. I tell him not to go out on the bike when he has been drinking. But he doesn't listen to me I am not sure what to do." replies Mom.

"Well, Mrs. Monroe there will be a hearing to determine how long of a suspension that Mr. Hill will receive. He will have to post bail. He is down at the jail house now waiting for the judge to set bail for him" explains the officer

The officer gave Lisa's mom his card. She closed the door and went back to the table to finish her dinner, Lisa had cooked. Lisa could tell that her mom was upset and she didn't want to say much so when her mom was finished her dinner Lisa grabbed the plates and took them to the sink where she cleaned up after supper.

"How could he be so stupid and so immature to do this? He knows that if he does something like this he's going to get caught," says Mom.

Lisa with her back turned, had a grin on her face she was quite proud of what she had done by calling the police and getting Scott arrested on DUI charges, after she had finished laughing to herself she turns to her mom and says.

"He does this because he knows you're going to bail him out. You have done this before and I have had no food or money for school I think he needs to learn his lesson and stay there until someone else can bail him out. Maybe one of his biker buddies can do it," replies Lisa

"You're right; I am tired of cleaning up his crap all the time, when he gets out of jail he is going to get a job and work for a living, maybe I can stay home and be with you a little more. I mean look at, you your skin and bone and your clothes are dirty I feel so bad I have been neglecting you for a long time. You're a very pretty girl and pretty girls need to have pretty things. Now I know your life hasn't been the best and I am seeing that now. But I am trying my best to give you what you want," explains Mom.

"Well I am tired and I am off to bed I have school in the morning. Good night mom," Lisa says

Lisa goes to her room, shuts the door behind her and locks it. She gets out a dirty pajama shirt and changes into that for bed Lisa gets in her bed the only place that she feels secure she goes to sleep. In the morning Lisa gets up before the alarm went off. She got dressed in the cleanest clothes that she could find a T-shirt and a pair of jeans with rips in the knees. Lisa comes out of her bedroom and heads to the kitchen where her mom is sitting. Her mom was on the phone and breakfast was on the table, a bowl of cereal and the milk sitting beside it.

Lisa sits down and pours the milk on her cereal, but the milk is clumpy it went sour Lisa gets up and heads out the door with a bagged lunch that her mom had made for her. The school bus came Lisa got on. Again she headed to the back of the bus like she has done every morning and every afternoon for years and she sits by herself on the bus.

When Lisa arrived at school she was met by Mrs. Kay who was not impressed that Lisa skipped detention the other day. Mrs. Kay had her arms crossed she was tapping her foot on the ground when she seen Lisa. Lisa didn't see her. she was focused on something else, but when Mrs. Kay spoke, Lisa literally jumped out of her skin. When she heard her name being called.

"Miss Monroe nice to see you today," growls Mrs. Kay.

"Oh, hi Mrs. Kay, I didn't see you there," responds Lisa.

"Don't get smart with me. You saw me you were just avoiding me. You, Young lady are, heading straight to the principal's office for skipping detention" angrily replies Mrs. Kay.

Lisa hung her head in shame and then thought to herself with a sad look on her face, *Mrs. Jones oh brother this should be fun sitting in her office. Should I make a run for it? Or should I face my punishment? I know I will wind up getting a suspension and if mom finds out, I am grounded. Oh boy this is going to be rough'.*

"Right this way dear, Mrs. Jones is waiting for you." says Mrs. Kay.

Lisa walks into Mrs. Jones's office with her head hanging down like she already knew what her punishment was going to be. Mrs. Jones closes the door and walks about her office admiring her things that students have given her over the years, then she grabs her chair and sits in front of Lisa.

"Okay let's get right down to business Miss Monroe, you know why you're here don't you?" asks Mrs. Jones.

"Yes I skipped detention" replies Lisa in a soft voice.

"Very good now, why did you skip detention?" asks Mrs. Jones

Lisa looks at Mrs. Jones with tears in her eyes; she was trying not to cry she clears her throat sits up straight looks at Mrs. Jones with her blue eyes, Lisa began to speak.

"I skipped because I had to catch the bus if I missed the bus I would have an hours walk home and I had to be there to get supper for my mom and step-dad" explains Lisa.

"Dear I have heard that excuse before you need to do a lot better than that if you're going to fool me I have been an educator for way too long and I have heard all these excuses before so good try dear" responds Mrs. Jones.

"It's the truth I had to I am not fooling you Mrs. Jones I wouldn't do that not at all" says Lisa.

"Miss Monroe if you think for a minute that I am going to buy that poor excuse then you're a foolish child can't your step-father cook supper? That is why he is there" replies Mrs. Jones.

"If you knew what type of guy that he was you would have skipped detention too I am sure you would have" exclaims Lisa.

"Nice try dear I know for a fact that it's an excuse, what is done is done and now comes the consequences for your actions" says Mrs. Jones

Alone Volume 1

Lisa got a lump in her throat she knew what was coming it was a suspension she for sure would be grounded and would have to suffer the wrath of her mother as well Mrs. Jones.

"For your punishment you stay for detention today after school and a letter goes home to your mother, if you skip out again I will be forced to call your mother to have a talk with us, do I make myself clear" warns Mrs. Jones

"I will make sure the bus comes back and gets you the kids that have detention need to get home too so the bus comes back if that is what your worried about, while in detention you will redo that test since your mark wasn't the best on it" explains Mrs. Jones.

"So if you agree I will send you back to class" says Mrs. Jones.

"Okay I will stay after school and do this test as part of my punishment" replies Lisa.

Lisa headed back to class she looked at the clock and was shocked for how long she was in Mrs. Jones office, *'Two hours in the office that was brutal I have missed half of class this sucks'* Lisa walks into Mrs. Kay's class the students were busy working Lisa just walked in sat down and began to work on the class was working on, with only a short time before lunch Lisa got done what she could the rest she would have to do at lunch time while she was eating her lunch.

The lunch bell ran and the students ran out of the room Lisa got up and Mrs. Kay stopped her before she left class.

"I don't like being interrupted you know to check in just don't come and sit down without saying your back is that clear" warns Mrs. Kay.

Lisa went to the court yard sat and ate her lunch it was a beautiful day to and Lisa took full advantage of it, the lunch that her mom had made for her was a peanut butter and jam sandwich and a soda pop to drink, because Lisa had no breakfast she was super hungry and ate the sandwich quickly.

The after lunch bell rang Lisa gathered her stuff and headed back to class feeling satisfied from lunch Lisa made her way to the class room she went inside and took her seat and had her books out on the desk, one other student came in after her a boy he stared at Lisa and then started to speak to her.

"Your always here early and the first one in class too" replies the boy

"I don't have anyone to hang with I have no friends and any friends I do have never stay around long enough to get to know me "says Lisa.

"Then there not good friends then" replies the boy

"My name is Rick, Rick Bell I know your name already its Lisa right?" asks Rick

"Yes, it is, "replies Lisa

This is was the first time that anyone had spoken to Lisa in a while she had seen Rick in her class but never knew who he was, the rest of the class started to file in then Mrs. Kay came in the class got right to work on math without any arguments the afternoon went fast Lisa had looked at the clock and it was almost time for home but she wasn't going home right away she had to do that test again, the bell rang and Lisa was the first one out the door and ran down the hall to the detention room she wanted to be over and done her detention she hated it, she grabbed the test sat down to rewrite it this time it was easier for her and she got the test done quickly and just in time for the bus.

Lisa ran out the door sprinting down the hall out the door to the school bus, Lisa got on just in time before the bus left, she headed to her usual spot.

When she arrived at home her mom's truck was in the driveway Lisa walks in and her mom was sitting on the couch watching TV.

"Hi Mom I am home" says Lisa

"How was school?" asks Mom

"Oh you know same old a boy spoke to me today I was shocked he seemed nice he is in my class he has been all year I just met him today" explains Lisa

"A boy good for you I am proud of you" says mom

Lisa went to her room to put her bag down when she came back out her mom was off the couch and in the kitchen,

"You know dear I didn't realize the that house was in such a mess I am going to quit one of my jobs I got a raise at my first one and with the two jobs and the extra money that I am getting we can get out of this place and move to a better one" says mom

Lisa feeling kind of sceptical about all this looks at her mom and asks.

"So what about Scott is he still in jail?" asks Lisa

"I don't know I haven't heard anything from anyone as far as I know he is but I am done with him I truly am done with him" says mom.

Lisa sat in front of the TV as her mother cooked, she was feeling relaxed when she heard the sound of a motor bike pulling she got a lump in her throat as she knew it was Scott was he going to do when he walked and seen Lisa and her mom home together.

Scott walked into the trailer he looked like crap he thumped into the kitchen and start to argue with Lisa's mom.

"So you thought you could keep me in jail hey well you have to do better than that if you want me to stay away" replies Scott

"I want you to leave you're not welcome here anymore until you can find a job and retain it for six months quit the beer and start helping out then you can come back but till then no get out" yells mom. Scott storms off outside getting into a black van, and leaving Seeing the demise of her mother and Scott Lisa, wonders what is going to happen, will Scott change and get a job or will he, be the same man that he has been for most of Lisa's young life Lisa, didn't really want to find out what, was going to happen to Scott, she was just happy that her mom had got rid of him and, that it is just the two of them.

"So what is next mom, now that Scott is gone?" asks Lisa

"We are going to move on, with our lives, I have lived to along in fear, of him and now that he is gone, we can be together, you and I we need to find a different place to live I have been looking at some apartment, that are nicer then this god dam tin can of a home, we can start over there, just you and I and maybe I don't have to work three freaking jobs to make ends meet" explains Mom

Alone Volume 1

Chapter 2

The next day, while Peggy happened to be, home early trying to get the place cleaned up so that they could move, a motor bike rides up, Lisa looks out the window and see's that is it is Scott, Lisa runs quickly to her bedroom and hides in the closet, she knows that there is going to be a huge argument between him and mom and Lisa, wants no part of this fight

"You want me out and to get a job come on Peggy you know I have nowhere to go," yells Scott

"You should have thought about that before you got, drunk and left on your bike," yells Peggy.

"If it wasn't for the retard, I know dam well she reported me and when I get my hands on her she, will pay for what she did to me," yells Scott.

"Don't you dare call her a retard, she is not a retard. She is a human with feelings," cries Peggy.

Scott leaves, the kitchen and storms, down the hall to Lisa's room she heard everything that's said, by this time Lisa was sitting in her closet with the door closed and is crying, She can hear Scott pounding on the door and her mom screaming at Scott not to do go through with putting your hands on her" cries Peggy

"Lisa I know you're in there. Open this door or I will kick it in," threatens Scott Lisa hid further into her closet frightened with fear Lisa prays nothing will happen things were quite for a minute then suddenly her bedroom door creaks she knew Scott had gotten into her room.

"Lisa I know in here come out I want to talk to you" says Scott

"Go to hell I have nothing to say to you" yells Lisa

"I asked you nicely to come out I wasn't rude to you please Lisa come out so that we can talk" pleads Scott.

Lisa sat there for a moment thinking if she should come out this was the first time that Scott had ever spoken nice to her usually it is an insult of some kind Lisa opens her closet door and emerges from her closet scared of what Scott might do to her she coward away from him.

"Come on Lisa I am not going to hurt you I just want to talk to you" says Scott.

"You can talk with me standing where I am at I am not moving from this spot and you can't make me move" says Lisa.

"Your right I can't make you move but I can force you to move and I want to talk to you face to face" pleads Scott. Lisa doesn't trust Scott she moves slowly to the corner of her bed Scott is standing with his arms crossed with his biker vest on and his boots and his fingerless biker gloves on.

"Nice to see that you are able to look at me face to face now why did you do it?" asks Scott

"Do what, what did I do" replies Lisa.

"Come on Lisa you know dam well what you did and I want to know why you did it" demands Scott

Lisa sat on the edge of her bed with Scott looking at her he was waiting patiently for her response. Scott moves closer to her as well, he could see that Lisa, isn't sincere and he wants an apology from her

"I am starting to lose my patients with you Lisa I know you were the one to call the cops and me arrested and I want to know why and I will stand here all night and wait for you to give me an answer" orders Scott.

"So what if I did what are you going to do, about it, you can't put your grubby hands on me, or you will end up right back to where you were, in jail" says Lisa

"You think you can order me around like that you don't care if I am around I heard everything outside between you and my mom she doesn't want you in the house and I don't either your lazy, your fat and you don't want to be bothered to get off your ass and do anything you make my mom do all the work and pay all the bills so that you can ride your motor bike, drink beer and listen to your music" says Lisa

"So is that what you think of me then hey well I have done a lot for you I took you to school once and a while I cooked your supper for you I did your laundry and this is how you repay me by telling me that you don't like me and that you too want me out of the house" explains Scott.

"That's right we want you out and get a job" replies Lisa.

"You are as stupid as you look you know that Lisa" yells Scott.

"I may be stupid but at least I do something about it I go to school you just sit on your fat ass and do nothing" snaps Lisa.

"Oh your cursing for an ass kicking girl you're getting pretty mouthy aren't you, Lisa maybe I should give you that ass kicking you deserve it you mouthy little brat" replies Scott.

"Why don't you kick my ass then, you seem to like to put your hands on women, I am just a child I can get you for abuse" laughs Lisa

"Oh you think this is funny don't you, you won't find it funny when I kick your ass" screams Scott

"I am not getting mouthy I am just sticking up for myself and for my mom" responds Lisa.

"Now leave me alone I don't want to be bothered" replies Lisa.

Scott was annoyed with Lisa's attitude he steps back slams Lisa's door stomps down the hall to his room where he sleeps and was throwing things around in the room Scott went to the hall closet to fetch his suitcase he packed all his clothes in the bag phone one of his biker buddies that has a truck to come and get him and his bike Scott will get a job and prove that he can do it.

Scott's friend shows up to pick him up Lisa was watching from her bedroom window watching Scott load his suite case and bike into his friend's truck.

As soon as Scott was out of the trailer park Lisa walked to the front room where her mother was sitting in tears and watching TV.

"Mom are, you okay?" asks Lisa.

"Yes I will be okay honey I was so afraid that Scott was going to hurt you he was so mad" says Lisa's mom

Alone Volume 1

Peggy Monroe was looking down at the ground as she talked to Lisa; Lisa was concerned for her mom she walked around to the front of the sofa and looks at her mom.

"Mom did he hurt you again?" asks Lisa

Mrs. Monroe looked up at her daughter with her eye swollen shut and blood coming from her nose.

"What an idiot he has no right to do this to you mom cries" Lisa.

"I was only trying to protect you if he would have gotten his hands on you god only knows what he would have done to you" replies Peggy.

Lisa went to the bathroom ran some water for a facecloth and came to the living room to help her mom Lisa wiped the blood from her nose then went to the kitchen to get an ice pack for her mom's eye.

Lisa sat on the couch beside her mom for a bit then she decided to go to bed as she was heading to bed she locked the dead bolt on the door and the knob and put the chain across the door in case Scott came back to the house tonight to try something. Lisa heads to the bathroom to brush her teeth and have a shower with a clean pair of pajamas on she went to her room closed the door locked and climbed into bed for the night.

Lying in bed Lisa thought about what Scott had said about her calling the police and wondered if she should tell her mother of what she had done.

Lisa went to sleep thinking that she would tell her mother in the morning if she was in the mood to hear it.

Lisa's alarm went off she rolled over to shut it off, Lisa sits on the edge of her bed trying to focus her eyes from the nights slumber she got up opened the curtains went to her dresser and found a t-shirt and a skirt to wear to school it looked warm outside and Lisa was tired of wearing jeans.

When she walked out her room Lisa went straight to the kitchen where her mom had breakfast cooked and on the table.

"Morning Lisa how was your sleep?" asks Mom

"Fine mom it was fine" replies Lisa.

Alone Volume 1

"What's wrong Lisa you seem unhappy this morning I don't see why it's a nice day out and it's you and I together" says Mom

Lisa sat there silent for a minute fighting back the tears of what she did she looks at her mom and says.

"Mom I am responsible for getting Scott in trouble with the police I feel so guilty that I did that and I am terribly sorry for it mom" cries Lisa.

"I am not mad at you for that I kind of already figured it out I am more disappointed that he did that I am not disappointed at you I love you Lisa" replies Mom.

Lisa ate her breakfast of French toast, orange juice once she was done she put her plate in the sink grabbed her back pack, kissed her mom and left the house to catch the bus, Lisa waited outside the trailer for the bus to come she could see it coming down the road to her stop the bus stopped in front of the trailer Lisa got on walked to the back and sat down.

When the bus pulled up to school she got off the bus walking into the school, Rick the boy she met yesterday was waiting for her at the door.

"Good Morning Lisa how are, you this morning?" asks Rick

"Oh I am good how are, you?" ask Lisa.

"I am okay this morning Lisa" responds Rick.

Lisa not used to conversation tried to find the words for Rick, Lisa looked at him and smiled at him as she walked to her locker, Rick was coming down the hall toward her locker Lisa, was hurrying to get into class, Rick stopped her and asks.

"Would you like to go for, a milkshake sometime I know a great place that serves the best shakes and fries?"? Asks Rick.

At a loss of words, Lisa fumbles with her words speaking in gibberish trying to think of something to say to Rick.

"Sure I would like that" replies Lisa.

"Great when would you like to go with me"? Asks Rick

"Oh it doesn't matter whenever you want" says Lisa

"Good how about today, we go directly to the place and then I walk you home" answers Rick.

Alone Volume 1

"I do have to ask my mom, first if it's alright I can get her to pick me up" says Lisa.

"Call your mom, I don't mind walking you home, my parents don't care if I tell them what I am doing and where I am going too" says Rick

Rick and Lisa went to, class together Lisa felt a little uncomfortable having a boy walk her home, Lisa thought

'I really don't want him to walk me home to where I live I am ashamed that I am living in the run-down trailer with shot up cars and garbage laying around, he seems nice no one has ever been nice to be before thought Lisa.

The morning bell rang; class was in session the students all waited for Mrs. Kay to come in the class. Mrs. Jones walks in with the books that Mrs. Kay uses for her lessons.

"Good morning class" says Mrs. Jones

The class looks straight ahead, not saying anything to Mrs. Jones

"Mrs. Kay unfortunately won't be here today and I am not sure about tomorrow, until I find a sub for this class I am in, charge of all you" demands Mrs. Jones.

Lisa thought to herself when she seen Mrs. Jones *'Oh great this was going so good a boy talked to me I was happy, now I am not my, worst nightmare is here'* thought Lisa

The seemed to go by fast, Mrs. Jones was in and out of the class dealing with students that were, being bad Lisa looked at the clock and watched the minutes tick by for lunch, when the lunch bell rang, Lisa grabbed her books and started to head out the door, Rick was behind her with his books in his, hand he stops Lisa at her locker and says.

"Do you want to have lunch, together"? Asks Rick

Lisa paused for a moment, unsure of what to say she didn't want to say no but she likes her lunches to herself.

"Sure let's have lunch together today Rick" replies Lisa.

So, walking to Lisa's lunch spot in the school courtyard the two find a seat they sit down and start eating lunch and Rick starts talking to Lisa.

"So this area is nice, I usually just sit in the cafeteria and have lunch" says Rick.

"I go there sometimes most of the time I have a bag lunch that my mom makes for me" replies Lisa.

"You seem a little; nervous am I making you nervous"? Asks Rick

"No I am not used to hanging with people I am kind of an outcast so I keep to myself" explains Lisa

"I don't understand why your, an outcast your very pretty and kind" compliments Rick

Lisa blushed a little bit, when Rick said she was pretty that made her feel good.

"Did I embarrass you"? Asks Rick.

"No I have never had a boy think I am pretty" replies Lisa

"Well I think you are I would like to be your friend if you would let me" suggests Rick.

"Why me there are lots of other girls in the school, that are cuter then me, why not them"? Asks Lisa.

"I picked you because I like you Lisa all these, other girls aren't like you, you're different but I can't put my finger on it" says Rick

"Different how? Stupid different or what is it that makes me so different from the other girls"? Asks Lisa

"Well first you're not stupid, and second I chose you because I think you and I can, are good friends" explains Rick.

Rick did most of the talking Lisa soaked it all in as Rick chattered, the bell rang again to head back to class, Lisa got up off the ground Rick ran and grabbed the door for her, Lisa not used to this pampering is a little taken back by the kindness of Rick, *'I can't understand what it is he likes in me, I am not the smartest girl but yet he is being so kind something that, I never thought that guys could be that nice thought Lisa.*

The afternoon classes consisted of Mrs. Jones giving lectures to the students Rick was sitting three rows from the right of Lisa and was looking over at her while Mrs. Jones spoke.

Alone Volume 1

'I sure like Lisa, I wonder if she feels the same way about me, am I coming on to strong, should I kind of take a step back, god I am not sure what I should do' thought Rick.

Lisa again watched the minute's tick by she was, wanting to get this nightmare over with having Mrs. Jones as the teacher, the end of school bell rang and Mrs. Jones dismissed the class, Rick followed Lisa out to her locker as she grabbed her back pack.

"You ready"? Asks Rick

"Oh yes I have to call my mom" replies Lisa

Lisa heads to the front of the school to the office to use the phone.

"Hello Mom" says Lisa

"Hello sweetie" replies mom.

"I am going to be late coming home; I was asked to for a shake with a boy" explains Lisa.

"Is this the boy you spoke of?" asks Mom

"Yes, it is mom" answers Lisa.

"Okay well don't be late I need you home I can come pick you up you let me know where you are at" says Mom.

"Okay mom, I love you" says Lisa

Lisa hung up and her and Rick walked to the place where, he hangs out to have a shake the place was called Peggy Sue's a popular hangout for the kids to have milkshakes and fries, Lisa and Rick entered the small diner heading to Rick's usual table both sat down and waited for their order to be taken.

"Hello Rick how are you doing today"? Asks Peggy Sue

"I am good" replies Rick.

"And who is this young lady that you have with you"? Asks Peggy Sue

"Peggy Sue this is, Lisa she is in my class" replies Rick.

"She's adorable Rick and a keeper if I say so myself" compliments Peggy Sue.

Peggy Sue takes the orders Lisa just ordered a, Vanilla Milkshake, Rick ordered a whole meal.

"See I told you that this place was great didn't I" gloats Rick.

"Yeah it's great" hesitates Lisa.

Alone Volume 1

"What's with the hesitation you seemed happy earlier"? Asks Rick.

"Oh not much just nervous and a little shy that's all" replies Lisa.

"A little shy you don't seem shy at all to me" responds Rick.

"You don't know how much I appreciate your kindness Rick but how on earth am I going to pay you back for such a treat" wonders Lisa

"Don't you worry Lisa, I wanted to do this for you, like I said I like you" says Rick.

Rick and Lisa sat, at the diner drinking their milkshakes. When the two were done Lisa phones her mom to come and get her from the, diner mom obliges she has some news for Lisa, Lisa and Rick waited outside for Miss Monroe to come, she showed up in a beat up Chevy truck, Rick got a sense of what Lisa went through and what kind of person her mom, is

"So will I see you on the weekend Lisa"? Asks Rick

"I don't go out on the weekends I stay home and do things at the house" replies Lisa.

Rick handed Lisa his phone number he looks at Lisa and says.

"If you want to hang sometime let me know" says Rick

Lisa Introduced Rick to her mom, Peggy Monroe was pleased to meet him but wanted to get home so that Lisa can hear the news that she had, for her.

"He seems nice" says Mom

"He is nice likes to talk" replies Lisa.

"Well if you like him that is the main thing" says Peggy

"So how long is this truck going to last for now mom"? Asks Lisa

"Well it cost me a week's wages to get out of the shop" replies Mom

When Lisa and her mom pulled up to the trailer they got out and went inside Lisa put her bag down and headed to the kitchen.

"So I have some news for you Lisa" says mom

"Really what is it?" asks Lisa

Alone Volume 1

"We are moving out of this tin can of a trailer I found an apartment close to work so that I am not driving the old truck to much" explains Mom

"Wow that's nice when do, we move?" asks Lisa

"Well we have to we have to go through our stuff most of this is Scott's stuff and this is trailer he is moving back in if we pack this weekend we can move in, its fully furnished so we just take our, clothes with us" explains mom

"And after we move in we are heading across to the bridge to New Jersey to see grandma" says Mom.

This was all too much for Lisa to absorb she headed to her room and started packing up the things that, were important to her, the suit cases were being placed at the door, once all the belongings were by the door they were loaded in the truck, Lisa and her mom put the key to the trailer in the mail box, and headed to the new apartment.

Finally, at the new apartment, Lisa and her mom carried stuff into the building to the second floor the building was older and the hall way smelt like gas and there were yellow stains on the ceiling where water had leaked.

"So what do you think Lisa?" asks Mom

"Well I think if the, building was better worked on it would be more attractive" answers Lisa.

"This is just the hall way wait till you see our unit, it was recently fixed up" says Mom.

"That's nice I can't wait to see it" says Lisa

They opened the door with all the bags at the door waiting to go in when Lisa's mom opened the door, Lisa walks in looks around turns to her mom and says

"I am impressed this is a nice unit" says Lisa.

"Told you it would be you have to trust me when I say I am going to, do something I will do it this is a fresh start for us" explains Mom.

"So Scott doesn't know where we live?" asks Lisa.

"No I never told him that we got this apartment all he knows is that we are in New Jersey at grandma's place" says mom.

Alone Volume 1

Lisa took her stuff to her new room, she stood in the door way of her room and looked around she walked in put her bags on her bed and started to go through the stuff she has and put things in their place.

"So you like your new room?" asks Mom

"It's nice" replies Lisa

"How could you afford this entire place mom, the new stuff and the apartment?" asks Lisa.

"I cashed in my 401k this is for us no more Scott, just us" replies Mom

"Well I am happy mom; we get to have a life together" says Lisa

After the move in was done Lisa and her mother got in the old beat up truck and headed to New Jersey to see Lisa's grandma, most kids they like grandma's place but not Lisa.

Lisa head to her, new room and started to unpack her suitcases the new apartment, was full of new furniture and, the walls were freshly painted, Lisa looks around in the new apartment, she likes what she sees, Lisa headed to the kitchen the kitchen was what she liked the most, it was small, but cute, Lisa loves to cook so this kitchen will, be nice for her, the kitchen has brand new counters and the counter tops were granite, a step up from what they were in before the tin can of a trailer that whenever the train rolled by the trailer shook, it leaked when it rained and got cold in the winter when it snowed.

"So what do you think, of the new place?" asks Mom

"I like it, I really do mom this is a fresh start for us" replies Lisa

"It is a fresh start for us, it's just you and I know more Scott and that is the way I want it, it's going to be hard but I think I will adjust to the fact that Scott is gone" says mom

Looking at the clock ticking on the wall and, the weekend coming fast Lisa and her mom decide what they want for supper, ordering Chinese food and sitting on the couch watching TV on this Friday night, Lisa and her mom enjoy the surroundings of the new place that doesn't smell like beer and cigarette smoke, the food finally arrived and, Lisa and her mother dug in this was from their favourite place to eat, feeling full Lisa heads to her room to fetch the cleanest night shirt she could find the jeans she had on were feeling tight from all the food she ate and her little seventy six pound frame felt like it had eaten an elephant, coming back. Lisa sits close to her mom, and the girls watch TV.

Chapter 3

Lisa always likes to hang with her mom but this trip to grandmas was, not something that she was looking forward too. Lisa and her mom drove the One hour and twenty-one-minute drive to Trenton New Jersey.

Once in Trenton Lisa sat looking straight through the cracked windshield of the old truck, once at the house of Lisa's grandma's place Lisa was trying to figure out where she was, this wasn't the place she had seen before, it was a different place Lisa felt creeped out by the look of the place that her grandma lived in garbage all over the place cars sitting in the parking lot with no tires or doors,

"Oh my god it's so good to see you my dears" cries Grandma

"And Lisa look at you, you have grown to be a pretty girl" compliments grandma.

Lisa looks at her with a smile her grandma had gotten older looking since last time she had seen her, Lisa and her mom walked into the house, it smelt like cigarette smoke and stale beer, something that Lisa was used to smelling.

"So what is new with my two girls?" ask Grandma

"Well, mom Lisa and I have moved to a new apartment by ourselves just us now no Scott" answers Peggy.

"Good move I never like him he's lazy, all he does is ride his motor bike and that is all makes you work all the jobs and pay the bills, you should have left him years ago" replies Grandma.

"And how about you Lisa how is school going, are you enjoying it?" asks Grandma.

"No I am, not school is hard and I am not making any friends except for this one boy named Rick, he is so nice and very dreamy too, we hung out the other day at lunch and he took me for a milkshake at his, favorite diner where all the kids hang out" explains Lisa.

"Well that is nice dear, you always were a shy kid always wondered if you were going to be something or be like your mother a hard-working woman, I can see that you might be your mother didn't like school" says Grandma.

The three women chatted about things, then the door opened it was a man; he had grey hair, skinny and held a bag with beer, and cigarettes.

"Oh Hank is back; Hank is that you" shouts Grandma.

"Yeah it is who the hell you think it is Santa Clause" yells Hank

"Do we have, company, Brenda?" asks Hank

"Why yes dear we do, it is Peggy and Lisa they have come to see us" replies Lisa's grandma.

"Oh well, that is nice have a good visit" replies Hank.

Hank is Brenda's boyfriend, after Peggy's dad died her mom began to date different men, Hank has been in her life now for ten years, unlike Scott Hank works Hank is an Auto Body Mechanic with a drinking problem, years of hard drinking has made him look older than he is.

The visit of Lisa's grandmother was going, not bad Lisa was kind of enjoying herself, after having some cake and a Pepsi to drink, Lisa and her mom decided to go shopping taking Lisa's grandmother with them,

"Hank" shouts Brenda.

"What the hell do you want now women?" asks Hank

"I am going shopping with Lisa and Peggy" says Brenda

"Why do you want to go, and spend money on stuff?" asks Hank

Coming out of the living room with a beer in his hand, and jeans hanging halfway down he sees Peggy and Lisa.

"Nice to see you again Peggy and Lisa" says Hank

"Like wise" replies Peggy?

"What the hell you so cold toward me for I didn't do anything wrong to you" shouts Hank.

Alone Volume 1

"I guess not but I have lots on my, mind I guess" replies Peggy.

"No Scott... I thought he would come I could modify is bike for him I love that bike" smiles Hank

"Scott and I aren't together anymore Hank, I was tired of his crap, Lisa and I have moved into our own place together just her and I" explains Peggy.

"Now why would you do that for, he was always nice to me" says Hank.

"You didn't have to live with him, he was a mean nasty man, the stuff I had to do when his biker buds came around, I didn't want to subject Lisa to the kind of the things that those awful men, wanted done" explains Peggy

"OH... hog wash I seen worse than that when I was Lisa's age, I seen things that no one should see" says Hank.

A former Vietnam War Vet Hanks rough and tough exterior was met, by his rough and tough personality.

"Well Hank if you like him so, much you can come see him he is living at the trailer now as far as I know, he doesn't know we have moved and would rather him not know that we have moved or where we are" replies Peggy.

Hank went back to the living room, with his beer in hand, the ladies headed out the door to the shopping mall.

"You still, have this old truck, I remember when you first got it" says Brenda

"Yeah it is getting old I just put a week's wages into it, but it made it here at least.

With a day of shopping and visiting, later that evening Lisa and her mom headed back to New York from Trenton making the One hour and twenty-one-minute drive again. It was dark when Lisa and her mom got to the apartment and upstairs, Lisa was tired she had done a lot of shopping with her mom and grandma.

"Well we are home Lisa" says her mom

"Thank god" answers Lisa.

"Come on now did you, not like your visit?" asks Mom.

Alone Volume 1

"I did, until Hank came in, I have never liked him" replies Lisa

"I know I, don't either but he makes your, grandmother happy so we kind of have to be nice to him" says Mom.

With a new wardrobe of clothes Lisa headed to her room to put her clothes away she thought for a moment if she should shut her door or leave it open, after all it was just her and her mom what was the big deal if she left her door open, she would decide after she was done with her clothes if she wanted to shut her door for the night.

"Lisa it's getting late, and you have school in the morning" calls Mom.

"Okay Mom I will be done here in a minute" replies Lisa

With the last of her clothes to put away Lisa shuts her door and locks it she continues to put her clothes away, once she was done, Lisa put on her clean pajamas pulled back the covers on her new bed and went to sleep.

In the morning when Lisa got up from the night's sleep, she headed out to the kitchen her mom was up and had breakfast ready and lunches made.

"Good morning how did you sleep?" asks Mom.

"Fine" answers Lisa

"Sit down and have breakfast, and get ready for school, I am taking you to school, I need to change the addresses on file" explains Mom.

Lisa got ready for school since her mom was taking her she didn't have to rush out the door, Lisa left the apartment with her mom and they went down the four flights of stairs to the parking lot where the truck is parked.

"I am working late tonight; you have your keys to get in I have left a frozen dinner in the freezer for you" says mom

"Okay that's fine I guess you have to work now to pay for, everything in the apartment" replies Lisa

"What is that supposed to mean huh Lisa" yells mom

"I never knew you had a 401k I thought you had put it all on credit that's what most people do don't they?" wonders Lisa.

Alone Volume 1

"Some people do, I have had a 401k for a long time it was always security for you and I, now that it is you and I, I had to use it" explains Mom.

Lisa and her mom arrive at the school; Rick awaits the arrival of Lisa. Lisa gets out of the truck with her mom behind her, Rick started walking toward Lisa and the two met halfway to the doors.

"Good morning Miss Monroe" says Rick

"Good morning Rick" says Peggy

"This was mighty nice you to meet Lisa at the door like this Rick, I am sure Lisa admires that, it shows you're a man" replies Lisa's mom

"Well, thanks Miss Monroe - "Please call me Peggy"- "Okay Peggy you see I really like your daughter" says Rick.

Lisa felt kind of embarrassed that Rick said what he did to her mom but none the less it made her feel good the things that Rick says makes Lisa feel good, Lisa and Rick headed to their lockers which were on opposite sides Ricks back was facing Lisa and was Lisa's back, while Lisa gathered her books for the morning one of the bullies that picks on her shows up.

"Hey nerd you going to stink up the classes again like you always do" degrades the bully, this time Lisa ignored the bully's teasing and walked away but he wasn't done he kept yelling obscene remarks to her until Mrs. Jones heard him.

"Jason Group, when are you going to learn not to bully, people around do we need to have a date in my office" warns Mrs. Jones very sternly

"No Mrs. Jones we don't need a date in your office" replies Jason

"Well then if I catch you again picking on Lisa Monroe, you will be in my office for the rest of the year do I make myself clear" demands Mrs. Jones

Jason didn't say nothing just walked to his class, which was down the hall from Mrs. Kay's room Lisa and Rick were in their seats Lisa was staring out the window as her mom sped off heading for work, Mrs. Jones walks into the class and walks up to the black board.

"Hello class" says Mrs. Jones

"I am here to let you know that Mrs. Kay is very sick and will not be back again today, her return is uncertain, so therefore I have found a sub for you all, say hello to Miss Veronica Appleton she will be the new teacher until Mrs. Kay returns" explains Mrs. Jones.

"Hello class nice to see you all, I will be happy to be your teacher" says Miss Appleton, Miss Appleton went around the room passing out the first assignment to the class it was an assignment, for her to get to know the students, she puts the paper down on Lisa's desk and smiles at her and continues to walk down her row passing out the assignment.

Once Miss Appleton gave the instructions to start working, the students began to do the assignment, it involved writing, and something that Lisa does when she writes in her journal at home, Lisa began the assignment pouring her heart out on the paper.

'The world just made a bit more sense to me today, I got rid of the bad guy in my life, Lisa went on 'he's not around to hurt me anymore and I feel good, the monster has hurt me for a long time with his words and with his fists, but now that the world makes a little more sense to me I realize that not all men are like that, I have met one that is so kind to me, and he said that he likes me a lot and I like that maybe the world isn't so cruel after all' Lisa was the first one done the assignment that was supposed to take most of the morning this was Miss Appleton's first day as a teacher and getting to know the students, Lisa put down her pen turned the paper over face down and sat and waited for Miss Appleton to collect the papers, Miss Appleton noticed that Lisa was done she causally walks over and collects Lisa's paper while genteelly putting her hand on Lisa's shoulder and walking back to the front of the class, Lisa looked at the clock that was in the only thing in the room that was making noise besides the sounds of pens or pencils scratching the paper or the sounds of students breathing.

The lunch bell finally rang and everyone headed out the door for lunch Lisa and Rick headed to the court yard again, it was windy outside the garbage that was in the can blew around in a small cyclone.

Alone Volume 1

"Windy today do you want to go in and hang out someplace in the school?" asks Rick.

"Yes let's do that I don't feel like sitting outside to eat lunch in this wind" replies Lisa.

Lisa and Rick headed to the inside area of the school where some of the kids eat lunch not wanting to, sit in the cafeteria Lisa and Rick sat in the hallway eating lunch.

"I was hoping we could have hung around on the weekend" says Rick

"We went to Trenton New Jersey to visit my grandma" replies Lisa

"Trenton wow that was a nice trip" replies Rick

"The only trip that, my mom and I ever take we don't get out much" says Lisa

"We get out all the time, we go to my grandmother and grandfathers cabin in the mountains, we go there often" explains Rick

"That's nice your family, must have money" replies Lisa

"Yes we do my mom is the District Attorney and my dad is a cop" says Rick

"Wow those are good jobs, ones that I will never be able to do" replies Lisa

"Never, say never," smiles Rick

Lisa and Rick sat and chatted until the bell rang for the afternoon session of class with Miss Appleton, they headed back to class Miss Appleton was already in the class sitting at her desk, as Lisa walked by Miss. Appleton looked at her but didn't say nothing Lisa sat down at her desk and took out her books.

"Lisa" calls Miss Appleton

"Before you take your books out I need to see you, once the rest of the class comes in, and I get them started you and I, need to have a chat" replies Miss Appleton.

Lisa looked at her, with wide eyes then she thought to her *'I wonder, what she wants, could it be the assignment that we, did I was only, saying how I felt.*

Alone Volume 1

The class came in and got seated Miss Appleton, then grabbed Lisa and they went for a walk to a little room that wasn't used very much.

"Lisa, Lisa, I cried when I read your assignment, it was very moving words, has this actually happened to you? Lisa or was, it just how you felt?" asks Miss Appleton

"It's actually how, I am feeling right now, the monster that I am referring to is my step dad Scott Hill, he wasn't a nice man he would hit me and use his words to make me feel, bad" explains Lisa.

"As your, teacher this concerns me" says Miss Appleton.

"You're a nice person, and everything Miss. Appleton but Mrs. Kay is my teacher you're a sub to us, no offence" expresses Lisa

"Lisa I am your, teacher now, I will let you in on secret you have to promise that you won't tell anyone" replies Miss. Appleton

Lisa with wide eyes looks at Miss. Appleton with a concerned look on her face.

"What do you mean your, the new teacher now" says Lisa

"Mrs. Kay is very sick and she will forced to retire before the year is up I am taking over her class and the next grade you will be in" says Miss Appleton

"So what you're, saying is that I am going to have to trust you, to teach me, then right"?" asks Lisa

"Yes you are going to have to work with me, I have looked at your work, you have a gift, I can tell by talking to you that you don't like school and you would rather be at home am I right?" asks Miss Appleton.

"That would, accurate to assume Miss Appleton, I have never liked school I just go because if, I don't my mom won't be happy, she never liked school herself, and I don't either her mom made her go, and now my mom is making me go" explains Lisa

"I will try to make your school experience fun, if there is anything you need anything at all, I will help you" offers Miss Appleton.

"I appreciate that, Miss Appleton, and if I need anything I will tell you" replies Lisa.

Alone Volume 1

"Here I am not supposed to but, if you need to talk, you can phone me at home" replies Miss Appleton

Miss. Appleton hands Lisa a piece of paper with her, number on it, Lisa puts it in her pocket, Lisa and Miss Appleton get up and head back to class, Lisa went back to her seat and did the afternoon exercise that Miss Appleton had assigned, Rick who was curios was, trying to get Lisa's attention, Lisa was concentrated on the assignment that she was, given.

Riiiiiiinnnnnnnggg!!! The 3:00 pm bell rang, to signal the end of the day, Lisa who had just finished the assignment, got up from her chair and headed out the door, with Rick following.

"Lisa" hollers Rick, Lisa looks at Rick with a smile, Rick smiled back and says.

"Can I walk, you home?" asks Rick or are you on the same bus as me?" asks Rick.

"You can, if you want I don't mind" replies Lisa

So Rick and Lisa rode the bus home together sitting side by side on the bus, Lisa is always used to sitting at the back of the bus by herself, not normally sitting with anyone, she rode until her new stop.

"This is my stop" says Lisa

"See you tomorrow in class" replies Rick

Lisa got off at her stop she crossed the street and headed into the apartment building where she had a climb up the steep stairs to her fourth floor apartment, Lisa got out her keys and opened the door, she quickly looked around the apartment to make sure that no one was around, than she shut the door and locked the dead bolt and turned on the TV to her favorite program, then Lisa went to the kitchen to fix herself a snack of ice cream, peanut butter and chocolate on top this is her favorite treat when her, mom is working, once Lisa made her snack she sat down on the couch again to watch TV.

During Lisa's TV watching the phone rang nearly scaring, the socks off of her.

"Hello"

"Hi sweetie, how was your day?" asks Mom

"Oh it wasn't bad" replies Lisa.

"Well I am working here at the bar tonight, so don't wait up for me, not on a school night okay Lisa" orders Mom.

"Yes mom, I know I will be in bed if I am tired" replies Lisa.

"Well okay, make sure you clean up after, yourself and I love you" says Mom

"I love you too mom" replies Lisa.

Lisa went back to watching TV she had, just got back into the program that she was watching, when the phone rang again.

"Well dammit, why the hell can't I be left alone" says Lisa to herself

"Hello"

"Hi Lisa, It's Rick, did I catch you at a bad time?" asks Rick

"No I am just watching TV and having my after school snack" replies Lisa.

"So the reason I called was to, see why you and Miss. Appleton had been gone so long, from the class?" asks Rick

"It was nothing really, just girl stuff that's all" answers Lisa.

"Are you sure, she seemed like she was concerned when she, called you" replies Rick.

"It was, nothing really, Rick" repeats Lisa

"Lisa you, don't have to hide secrets from, me don't be afraid I am not going to judge you, I like you why would I judge you" says Rick

"Most people do, judge me by the way I am, I can't help it, that's the way I am, I am not the person that most people think, I am" explains Lisa.

"That doesn't matter, to me what matters is on the inside, the feelings" says Rick

"That's sweet of you, to think like that of me" blushes Lisa.

"Well see you at, school tomorrow" says Rick.

"Yes you too have a good night" replies Lisa

Lisa hangs up the phone heads back to the couch to finish eating her treat, and watching her show.

It was getting on, to Lisa's bedtime she wasn't tired and it was still light outside, she decides to hop in the shower and get herself ready for bed, Lisa heads to her room empty's her pockets, gets out her pajama's and goes into the bathroom for her shower, this was something that Lisa wasn't really able to do in her old place, the hot water heater leaked and the bathroom was disgusting, this one was fresh and new Lisa has the shower hot the steam in the bathroom was enough for her to bare, when she was done with a towel around her, head and one around her skinny body, Lisa leaves the bathroom heading to her room to put on her pajama's once she was in her pajama's with the TV still on she heads back to the living room, to finish watching TV, she wasn't really tired so she decided to wait up for her mom.

Midnight and the deadbolt made a click startling Lisa then the door opened up it was Lisa's mom.

"Hi mom" says Lisa

"What are you still, doing up silly you should be in bed, it's a school day" replies Mom.

"I know I wanted to wait up for you, to come home to see how your, day was" says Lisa.

"Aww that is so sweet of you, now get to bed, I will come tuck you in" replies Mom.

Lisa heads to bed like her mother asked, she wasn't too far behind, Lisa's mom came into Lisa's room and tucked her daughter in.

"I am not working at the bar, tomorrow night so, I will be home when you get home, from school, but Friday night I will, be working so you're going to be alone, if you want Rick can come over, you seem to get along well" says Mom

With a, kiss on the lips and I love you from her mom, Lisa goes to sleep. With her window open, and the night breeze blowing in, Lisa sleeps very soundly, this was first time in a long time that she was able to sleep so well now, that things are good and her and mom are happy, in their new place and they don't have to deal with the pain in the neck Scott

Lisa was tucked in tight and sound to sleep, when she had heard the sounds of motor bikes coming close she, got up and headed to the window, the motor bikes were just going by, they didn't look like any of Scott's group but, in the dark it's hard to tell Lisa waited until the bikes were gone then she went back to bed, and went back to sleep, then every hour on the hour, Lisa woke up to every sound she heard, I guess sleeping sound wasn't for Lisa this time, finally, Lisa got up and went to the bathroom, *'Finally a bathroom doesn't smell like pee, and the smell of mold and a wobbly toilet that when you sit on it, it wobbles all over I am really starting to like this place thought Lisa.*

Chapter 4

In the morning when, Lisa got up her, mom was sitting in the kitchen on the phone; with someone on the table was breakfast for Lisa, orange juice, crispy bacon and scrambled eggs. Lisa sat down to start having breakfast when her mom got off the phone, she came to the table.

"Good morning Lisa, how did you sleep?" asks Mom

"I slept fine" replies Lisa.

"I cooked your favorite food here" says mom.

"Yes I know thank you but I have to ask you, are you working a different job to mom, because I don't think the bar pays for all this" questions Lisa

"If you must know yes I did, working in an office setting as an administrative assistant the bar job won't last forever, I am going to be quitting that job and spending more time with you" explains mom.

"That would be good, you and I together, but I worry though mom I had seen a motor bike at the school the other day that looked like one of Scott's biker buddies it was like, he was snooping around the school" explains Lisa

"If you see anyone, you tell me or Mrs. Jones Scott isn't supposed to know where we are at all do I make myself clear" orders Mom.

Alone Volume 1

Lisa ate her breakfast then got her back pack and headed out the door to the school, bus with a full stomach and a new day Lisa would try to get through the day with the new teacher, Miss Appleton is nice enough to Lisa, but Lisa believes that she is being too personal by handing Lisa her personal phone number.

The bus showed up and Lisa got on the bus Rick was sitting in his seat so Lisa sat beside him.

"Good morning Lisa" Rick says

"Morning Rick" replies Lisa

"You're looking pretty today, well your pretty all the time to me" compliments Rick.

"You must really care for me" says Lisa

"Yes I do care for you, like I said I like you" replies Rick

"But I don't know much more about you then what you have told me, you told me that your dad is a cop and mom is a lawyer and you have a sister, but that is it, it's like your mysterious and I like that" explains Lisa.

"If anyone is mysterious, it is you and I like that in you" says Rick

"I am mysterious, like that I am keeps people guessing what is going on with me" laughs Lisa.

Lisa is enjoying the rides to school, Now that Rick is on the bus they arrive at school once the bus was at a complete stop, Rick and Lisa get off and head inside Lisa at her locker and Adam at his locker the school bully Jason came back to Lisa again.

"So you, think you're so great that you had the principle sticking up for you the other day, well she is not hear to rescue you this time, and I would like nothing better than to punch you and hurt you" threatens Jason.

"Go ahead punch me I can guarantee that you will only, get on hit in on me and you will, on the ground rolling around in pain when I am through with you" laughs Lisa

"You're a funny girl do you really think I am that stupid?" asks Jason.

"Yes I do think that" sarcastically says Lisa.

"After school in the field, you and I will fight and we will see who the toughest is in the school if, you win I will respect you, I win then I will be the biggest thorn in your side" warns Jason

"Are you nuts Lisa, he wants you to beat him up just so that you can get suspended" reacts Rick

"He has been a thorn in my side all year besides he won't show up, I am not fighting him anyway I will make him go to the, field I will be on the bus going home" laughs Lisa.

Lisa and Rick enter the class room Miss. Appleton was already in the class room sitting at her desk with tears in her eyes.

She waited for the all the kids to come into the class as the last kid enters she closes the door of the class room walks up to the front of the class and sits on her desk.

"Good- - morning—class" sobs Miss. Appleton

"I- have – some bad news- to- tell- you" replies Miss Appleton.

Miss. Appleton sat there for minute wiping her eyes she took a drink of water and proceeded to tell the class the bad news that she received this morning.

"Your probably thinking I am a cry baby, but I found out some bad news this, morning, Mrs. Kay has passed away, she was very ill and in the hospital she passed away with her family by her side early this morning" explains Miss Appleton

Lisa raised her hand to ask a question to Miss Appleton Lisa looked like she wanted to cry she loved, Mrs. Kay.

"Yes Lisa" replies Miss Appleton.

"So are you, going to be our teacher for the rest of the year?" asks Lisa

"Yes I am, Lisa I have been assigned presently to this class for now, then next year they will have me in the next grade after that" responds Miss Appleton.

"But because of Mrs. Kay's passing there is only half day today for this class and the school, she was special to this, school" explains Miss Appleton.

Lisa felt crushed by the passing of Mrs. Kay someone that really cared about her, and she was gone, now she was going to have to, get to know Miss Appleton, she seems nice so far and Lisa is really liking her. Because of the classes being shortened Miss, Appleton passed around a sympathy card for Mrs. Kays family and the morning was a writing time Miss Appleton, gave the class another writing assignment, this one was to describe how the class was feeling about the passing of their former teacher.

Lisa got out her book to a blank piece of paper, and she sat there wiping away the tears from her eyes.

'Today I lost someone close to me, a lady who very much cared for me, she was a special person, and she will be missed, I guess I am really feeling just so sad of things that have gone on, the bulling and the being called, different names, it saddens me, that I have to go through this, we recently got away from the monster, but now I feel were dealing with a different monster, what I mean is that we moved recently into an apartment just mom and me, paid for by her 401k something that she worked hard to get, but I think it was something more though, I think it was another one of the monsters that affects my life, but I am too afraid to, ask what it is, so I will remain silent, until my theory is proven, for now I am signing off and until get the chance to write again hopefully some of these monsters will have, been defeated.

Lisa, was the first one finished, she put down her pencil and sat back in her, chair letting out a big sigh, Miss Appleton came over to get her paper, she smiled at Lisa and patted her on the shoulder, Miss Appleton headed back to her, desk with Lisa's assignment, then she headed to another desk for the other students assignment, once the other students were done, Miss Appleton just assigned some, free reading for the class, Lisa pulled out her, book that she had been reading, the free reading, time would take the class until the end of the sad school day not just for 8B Mrs. Kay's class but for the entire school.

While Lisa was reading she, could see that Miss Appleton was reading the, assignments that the class had done, her body language suggested the paper she was reading was Lisa's Lisa sat there for a while watching Miss Appleton from the top, of her glasses, Miss Appleton, put the paper down and pulled out another Kleenex from the package that was on her desk, Miss Appleton's mascara was running down her face, she was wiping it off of her tear stroked, face Lisa went back reading, so not to draw any attention.

Before the bell rang, the PA system comes on and Mrs. Jones starts to speak

"Attention all staff and students, today is a sad day for this school we have lost, a very special lady and my dear Mrs. Betty Kay, it is at this time that I let the school go early, in lieu of her passing, I urge all the students that if, they want Mrs. Kay's funeral, will be held in three days, so for the next three days the school will be closed, to mourn her passing, she was a big part of the school and she will be, sadly missed, phone calls have gone out to your parents to say why the school will be closed. Have a good staff and students and I would like to see you all back here in three days in the school gym for Mrs. Kay's funeral.

Once the bell, rang to signal the end of the, day a song played on the speakers, the song that Mrs. Kay really loved, "What a Wonderful World" By Louis Armstrong, as the song played, the girls in the hall ways shed tears of sadness Lisa, headed to her locker then to the place where, she sits to eat her, lunch. Rick had tracked her down and sat beside Lisa, Lisa just sat there with her knees to her chest, not saying a word, then she noticed Rick sitting there.

"You didn't have to come, Rick I was just thinking you would get on the bus" cries Lisa.

"I wanted to be here Lisa for you, it hurts me to know that Mrs. Kay is gone it also hurts me to see you hurting and if there is something that I can do for you, I will" says Rick.

'Your very kind, Rick that's why I like you, so much and I was wondering my mom is working late at the bar that she works at, and I was wondering if you, wanted to come over Friday night and be with, me until my comes home?" asks Lisa

"Yes I can, my dad is working the night shift and well my mom is out of town, for a few days, so yes I just have to tell my dad tomorrow that, I won't be at home for the evening he's usually pretty good about, letting me, go out" explains Rick

Alone Volume 1

The buses finally came to get the kids, Lisa and Rick got up and headed to the bus, that they ride on, Lisa found a seat she sat down next to the window and Rick sat beside her, this bus ride would be different today Rick and Lisa would be two of the last to be dropped off, Lisa and Rick settled in for the ride home.

Lisa sat looking out the window, Rick sat close beside her, Lisa turned to Rick with a smile on her face, the first time Rick has really seen her smile, and she looks at Rick and says.

"Rick you're the first boy I have ever had I mean I am only fourteen but, you're the only one that really cares about, me besides my mother and Miss Appleton she's nice" says Lisa

"Well like I said I like you too and I care about you a lot too, Lisa there is still a lot I don't know about you and would love to know you more" says Rick

"Well you will get your chance to know me, better tomorrow night or whenever you come over, to my house I will have supper on I am a good cook too" replies Lisa

"I look forward to it" smiles Rick

The bus dropped off Lisa at her apartment building, as she gets off the bus Rick looks on watching her go into the building, once she was out of sight the bus pulled away, Lisa entered the apartment, and set her bag down and headed to the kitchen for a snack, Lisa turned on the TV and had the TV playing while she, made her snack, with a plate of carrots, celery and green pepper with ranch dressing Lisa sat on the couch watching TV, for the rest of the afternoon Lisa sat around doing the chores that her mom asked her to do and doing her homework, she thought a lot about Rick.

When Lisa was done her homework she started cooking supper for her mom she knew she was going to be home, while Lisa was cooking supper her mom walks in through the door carrying her purse and few groceries for the house she saw Lisa cooking

"Hi honey how was your day?" asks Mom

"Fine" responds Lisa

"Just fine" replies mom

"We got off early today and we won't be back in school until Tuesday or Wednesday" explains Lisa

Alone Volume 1

"Why?" asks Mom

"Mrs. Kay passed away from her sickness, so the school is closed and Monday we go for her funeral at the school" says Lisa

"Oh that's sad, I am sorry you really liked her, you're going to have to get used to a new teacher now" says Mom.

"Already have she has been teaching us for a week now, her name is Veronica Appleton, she very nice and pretty too" replies Lisa

"That's good, I am happy that you're happy and how's Rick treating you?" asks Mom

"Absolutely awesome Rick is such a nice, guy and so caring, and sexy I guess" smiles Lisa

"Good one" laughs mom

Lisa was happy that her mom was, home but deep inside she still had that fear of Scott finding out where, they live now that bothered Lisa she didn't want to see Scott she was afraid of him. Lisa and her mom stayed up, and watched movies and talked about girl things and what plans that Lisa has for the summer that was only two months away.

At mid-night that night Lisa and her mom went to bed, it was late and Peggy Monroe had a late night shift at the bar and at the hotel as front desk clerk she was still working two jobs, to pay the bills.

Lisa was able to sleep without pulling the covers up over her head like she usually did but she still slept with her door closed behind her, she could hear the sounds of the cars driving by and even the odd transit bus, the light from the street, peaked through the curtains in Lisa's room.

In the morning, Lisa got up to fix her mom some breakfast, she works hard and deserves a breakfast, but when Lisa got up her mom's bedroom door was open and she was gone, Lisa looked at the time on the microwave it said 9:00 am Lisa had slept in and missed saying goodbye to her mother, still in a short night shirt and hair a mess from the night's sleep Lisa headed back to her room to put, her glasses on she wondered back to the kitchen where there was a note on the counter.

'Hey sweetie you, were sleeping sound, when I checked in on you and I thought I would let you sleep, you can have your friend

Alone Volume 1

Rick over I won't be home till tomorrow sometime I have the late night at the bar then I head over to the Hotel for the a shift there, keep the place clean and I will see you tomorrow sometime.

Love Mom.

Lisa headed to her room after she read the note from mom, Lisa sets out clothes on the bed as she prepares to have a shower, Lisa checks to see if the door is secure to the suite, feeling insecure when she is alone, she makes sure she makes the place secure, Lisa runs back to the bathroom, she takes off her night shirt and gets in the shower, feeling clean Lisa grabs her towel, with her bedroom being across from the bathroom she took a chance and walked to her room naked no one was around, so she could pull it off, Lisa grabbed some deodorant and put it on then she grabbed a light blue bra and put it on once she was dressed, Lisa headed out to the living room where she sat to watch some TV, she looks at the clock hanging on the wall,10:00 am then Lisa thinks to herself.

'Should I call, Rick or wait for him to call me I would really like to hang out as we talked about thought Lisa

Lisa picks up the phone and dials the number that Rick gave to her, the phone rang three times on the other end before someone picked up.

"Hello I am looking for Rick" says Lisa

"This is Rick, Hi Lisa" answers Rick

"So what are you doing today Rick?" asks Lisa

"I was thinking about calling you, you mentioned you wanted to hangout today and I have all day and night my parents are working they have left the house to me and my sister they, know I am going to hang with you, and they said I can stay at your place if you want that" explains Rick

"That's cool" says Lisa

"So what time do you want me to come over?" asks Rick

"As soon as you can its very quiet here" says Lisa

"Okay I will pack a bag and get on the bus to your building I know where you live so I will be there in one hour" replies Rick

"Okay just buzz unit #201, and I will let you in" explains Lisa

"Okay sounds good I will see you in one hour Lisa, bye" says Rick

"Bye sees you" replies Lisa

Lisa hung up the phone she headed to her room to pick up the towel and put it the laundry hamper then she headed to the kitchen and cleaned up a little bit, she got the apartment cleaned and organized Rick is one of those guys that looks like he would live in a nice house, and clean as well, the hour had passed and Lisa heard the buzzer go off she skipped to the pad on the wall and pushed the button, she waited for Rick to come upstairs, then there was a knock Lisa looks through the peephole and its Rick, she opens the door with a smile.

"I am so glad you made it come in Rick" says Lisa

Lisa closed and locked the door behind her as soon as Rick came in.

"Make yourself at home, Rick I will take your bag" says Lisa

"Thanks Lisa" says Rick

"So this is your humble home, nice place your mom must work hard to keep this place" mentions Rick

"She does yes I miss her when she is working so much and I worry about her too she works so hard and I am home alone here she gets home early Monday to Thursday then Friday, Saturday she works at the bar and the hotel as a front desk clerk, the rest of the week she works as an administrative assistant for an accounting firm here in New York" explains Lisa

"So I take it, it's just you and your mom no siblings or a father" wonders Rick

"Yeah it's just mom and me, my father I never knew him when I was just a baby, he took some acid and committed suicide by jumping off the bridge into the Huston River, then my mom started to date a guy named Scott Hill, a former heavy metal DJ and biker man" explains Lisa

"Where is Scott now?" asks Rick

"I don't know and I don't care where he is he and my mom spilt a month ago we moved so he wouldn't find us" answers Lisa

Alone Volume 1

Rick and Lisa began by just talking then after about an hour or so Rick asks Lisa a question.

"It's such a nice day outside, would you like to take a walk in Central Park?" asks Rick

"I would love too, to go to Central Park I haven't been there for a long time" replies Lisa

Getting ready Lisa grabs her keys to the apartment and grabs her purse out of the closet beside the door, leaving with Rick they head downstairs to the outside, while waiting for the bus to come Lisa and Rick stood beside each other there was an older lady with a cart sitting on the bench, as the bus pulled up Lisa and Rick got on paying for the ride to Central Park, Rick is right it's a nice day out and the trip to central park is nice Lisa doesn't have many friends especially ones that are boys, Lisa and Rick walk side by side sticking close to each other.

"Such a lovely place to be don't you think" says Lisa

"Lovely yes but you know what's lovelier?" asks Rick

"No tell me" says Lisa

"You" says Rick

"Me well I don't think I am that lovely, but thanks any" replies Lisa

"I have a feeling you don't like yourself very much" says Rick

"What makes you say that?" asks Lisa

"I say things like your lovely and stuff but you say don't think you are I wouldn't say that if I didn't mean" explains Rick

"Rick your very nice I like you, I have never been, oh how can I say this to you without sounding silly, I have never really had much self-confidence mainly because I have been picked on and bullied for most of my life, and life with Scott wasn't the best, he's the biggest reason I am the way I am, Rick I have to tell you that at night I sleep with the door closed and locked, because Scott would get mean with me he did hurt me in any way he would get mean with his words especially when he drank, the mental and emotional abuse that I received I just shut down and stopped believing that people are nice, like you so if I seem a little bit like I don't appreciate the compliments I do but it's I am in secure with people" explains Lisa

Alone Volume 1

"I understand, I will try and give you more compliments to make you feel better about yourself Lisa" says Rick, After spending some time at central park Rick and Lisa went back to Lisa's apartment, they climbed the stairs and Lisa opened up the suite.

"That was wonderful, thanks Rick" says Lisa

Rick headed to the washroom, Lisa turned on the TV and opened the blinds to let some light in she heard Rick come out of the bathroom, he came in and sat on the couch Lisa smiled at him she went to the fridge and grabbed a couple of Cokes and they sat down to watch an afternoon movie, sitting beside Lisa Rick opens his Coke and sets it on the end table beside the couch.

'This is so nice to spend time with Lisa, she is such a kind sole I really love her, I wonder though if I got closer to her and put my arm behind her head if that would freak her out, I don't want to come on to strong'

"So Rick what else would you like to eat, we have chips and cookies there is more pizza over on the cupboard from our order?" asks Lisa

"I am good if I eat any more my jeans will burst open and that is not something I don't think you want to see, just yet" laughs Rick.

"No I don't want to be scared for life, seeing you burst out of your jeans" says Lisa

'Actually on second thought I wouldn't mind seeing that, I am starting to, really like Rick and I have some feelings for, him but no who am I kidding he doesn't feel the same way, about me I am sure of it, but oh my god what if he does, like me, I am not sure how I feel about that, but hey if he asks me out, I may say yes' thinks Lisa.

"What are you thinking about Lisa you went quite for a minute?" asks Rick

"Oh not much just thinking I was thinking something perverted that's all" laughs Lisa

"Oh really perverted hey, what was the thought about" flirts Rick

"I will never tell that's for my knowledge only" replies Lisa

Lisa and Rick hadn't done much since he came, over just watch TV and talk; this is the first time that Lisa has had a boy over especially when her mom isn't home

"You must think I am kind of boring were not doing nothing" says Lisa

"I don't think your boring at all I like just sitting here talking and watching TV besides its early yet, it's only 3:00 pm" replies Rick

"Really holly crap It is, so what do you want to do, we can go out later on or, we can watch one of my fast pace action Steven Seagull movies" says Lisa

"You're a Steven seagull fan" says Rick very surprise

"Yes I am a huge fan of his movies, and he hot" laughs Lisa

"I love his movies too Lisa" says Rick.

Chapter 5

Rick scoots closer to Lisa who is staring straight at the TV he slowly puts his arm on the back of the sofa, behind Lisa's head Lisa flinches a little bit as Rick got comfortable, Lisa turns to Rick and asks.

"What are you doing Rick?" asks Lisa

"I was just getting comfy and I wanted to sit closer to you this couch is big and we felt spaced out" explains Rick

"I understand you're being romantic, I like that" flirts Lisa

"I am only fourteen though Rick" says Lisa

"I am as well Lisa" replies Rick

"If you don't want, me to have my arm, behind you, I understand" says Rick

"No I am okay with it, remember it's not you it's me I like you" says Lisa

"I like you too, I guess I just have never gone through what you have, I have a good life at home I have two parents and siblings, I just have to try and understand" explains Rick

"Oh Rick I appreciate you loving me like this I really do like it" gloats Lisa

Alone Volume 1

It was late afternoon and the movie was over Lisa looks at the clock ticking away on the wall it showed 4:30 pm.

"Well time for me to, get some supper are you hungry Rick?" asks Lisa

"You said you're a good cook I am waiting to taste your cooking would you like some, help with the cooking" offers Rick

"You can if you want but I am okay you can sit at the breakfast and watch me cook if you want" says Lisa

"That would be lovely, I would like that" replies Rick

Lisa gets up from the couch and heads to her bedroom for a moment she put on a pair tight spandex pants that she had in her dresser, she came back out and Rick was sitting up at the nook.

"You changed your pants why?" asks Rick

"To be sexy for you" laughs Lisa

"You are sexy you don't have to be sexy for me when you are already a pretty girl" compliments Rick

"You do know how to make a girl so happy don't you and when I am with you, I am happy I guess this is what love feels like" says Lisa

"Love, are you coming around now Lisa?" asks Rick

"Perhaps I am coming around and coming out of my shell a little bit" replies Lisa

"I mean I did just put on tight pants for you" teases Lisa.

"Yes I see that, and I like what I see" smiles Rick

Lisa was in the kitchen cooking what she was cooking is surprise for Rick, Rick sits on the stool at the breakfast nook and watches as Lisa cooks.

"It smells good so far I am looking forward to it" compliments Rick

"Yes it does smell good, I am even getting hungry to eat it" says Lisa

As Lisa was cooking the door to the apartment opens and it's her mom

"Mom I thought you were working tonight" says Lisa in surprise

46

Alone Volume 1

"I am I got off early and I wanted to come home for supper" explains Mom

"Hello Mrs. Monroe" says Rick

"Hello Rick nice to see you again, I hope Lisa is being a good host and you kids are behaving" says mom

"Yes we are" replies Lisa

"I am going to have a shower and change then we can talk after that" says Mom

"I am hope she's okay with me staying the night" worries Rick

"I think she will let you stay the weekend with me" says Lisa

Mrs. Monroe returned a short time later dressed for the bar shift and had a change of clothes for the hotel shift supper was finally ready Lisa a had made a chicken stir fry with rice, Rick sets out three plates on the table, as Lisa dishes up the food into a bowl.

With a bowl of rice and the stir fry Lisa Rick and Peggy sit down to eat

"Mmm smells good Lisa" says Mom

"I hope it tastes as good as it smells replies Lisa

"So Lisa I am working until Sunday I have Monday off and are you going to be okay on your own?" asks Mom

"Well I was going to ask if you mind that Rick stays the night or if he can stay the weekend with me" inquires Lisa

"It has to be okay with his parents, but I am sure staying the night wouldn't be an issue" says Mom

"I told my parents who are away for the weekend that, I will be staying here with Lisa at least for a night or two so their okay with it as long of course we behave" explains Rick.

"Well if your parents said it's okay then I will, allow you two to spend the weekend here together" says Mom

When dinner was finished Rick and Lisa gathered up the dishes and took them to the sink as Peggy got ready to leave for her shift at the bar, Peggy made sure things were okay before she left with the kids, doing the dishes Peggy gets her shoes on and grabs a coat.

"Bye have a good weekend see you sometime Sunday" says Mom

"Yes bye Mom I love you very much have a good shift" calls Lisa

"Bye Rick thanks for staying with Lisa this is mighty nice of you" replies Peggy

"Your welcome Mrs. Monroe, see you" answers Rick.

As soon as Peggy left, Lisa and Rick finished up doing the dishes and have things put away, Lisa then heads to the living room to sit down and turn on the TV again Rick sat on the couch beside her, Lisa pulled out her ponytail that she had in and let her hair fall.

"Wow your hair is so long I have never seen without a ponytail before" says Rick

"I take my hair out at night if I don't it gives me a headache, my mom is jealous that I have longer hair then her" smiles Lisa

"My sister's hair isn't even that long and she would be jealous as well" says Rick

"How old is your sister?" asks Lisa

"She is sixteen and I have another sister who is twenty one, and she is in school to become a cop for NYPD" says Rick

"Wow that is awesome" says Lisa

"How about you do you have any career plans or ideas for when you're done school?" asks Rick

"I just want to get through junior high before I make any plans, but if I had to choose I would be a nurse or something I don't know" says Lisa

"Well you must have some kind of hopes and dreams for your future" replies Rick

"I always thought I would be married with two kids living in a sub division of New York and having my man take care of me

"Well that's a good start I mean I do like you and I hope that we can be boyfriend and girlfriend" hints Rick

"Are you asking me out Rick?" says Lisa

"Yes I am asking you to be my girlfriend" replies Rick

Lisa fell silent for a moment thinking to herself *'I can't believe he asked me out I mean why me there are other girls in school that he can have, but he chooses the most insecure person in the school and the shyest person too, but hey he asked me out so I will give him a shot what do I have to loose 'thought Lisa.*

"Yes I will be your girlfriend but just one thing Rick" answers Lisa

"What is it?" asks Rick with concern on his face

"Why did you pick the most insecure, the shyest person in school when you can have any girl in that school, you choose me, now I know what you're going to say and I just wanted to know why" explains Lisa

"Well I chose you because I don't just want some girl that is going to date me because I am good looking and smart, I want to date someone that is mysterious and not a girly girl, I mean you're not that type Lisa and that's what I love about you" explains Rick

"Wow you love me, I love you too I mean you have been so kind to me and I have been such a bitch, to you by trying to turn you away, but as I explained to you, that I am insecure and that is why I stay away from the other students and keep to myself" says Lisa

"You haven't been a bitch, yes you have been a little shy around me and I didn't understand why, just because you just have your mother raising you and you don't live in upscale New York doesn't bother me as I said like mysterious" says Rick

"I thought that is what all the boys liked the fact that a mother and father raise you and that you don't live in a trailer where you're afraid that the roof is going to blow off it when the wind blows or putting buckets in the hallways to keep the carpet from getting wet in the rain when the roof leaks" says Lisa

"That kind of stuff doesn't mean anything to me it's what is on the inside that count" says Rick

"So your just not dating me to get in my pants right?" asks Lisa

"No I am not I mean when you're ready we can but no not now" replies Rick

"I am only fourteen I mean I am old enough to know what men and women do and well I always thought that I would to have it" explains Lisa

"So you're saying you're ready then is that correct" replies Rick

"Not just yet let's give it sometime together as boyfriend and girlfriend before we jump in the sack okay" says Lisa

"Deal I will wait and I respect that, but one thing" says Rick

"What is that" replies Lisa

"Can I hug you at least and kiss you until were ready?" asks Rick

"Umm, no" laughs Lisa

"Of course you can silly I like kisses and hugs" flirts Lisa

"Oh good you had me worried for a moment" laughs Rick

Lisa gets up from the couch and heads to the kitchen for another coke she comes back and gives on to Rick

"It's 8:00pm on a Friday night, what do you want to do now?" asks Lisa

"What do you have planned do you go out much at night" replies Rick

"Not really I am kind of a home body watch TV and go to bed usually but it's Friday night , if you have something planned we can do what you want" says Lisa.

"Do you like sports?" asks Rick

"I do sometimes depends on what I am watching like hockey the New York Rangers and I like the Yankees why what do you have in mind?" asks Lisa

"Friday nights I hang out at the fight clubs down town and take in some of the boxing and the amateur wrestling" answers Rick

"That sounds fun when do they start?" asks Lisa

"Well if we catch the bus now we can go and take in amateur boxing match at my favorite fight club this one is in the Bronx" explains Rick

"The Bronx that is dangerous at nights a lot of people get hurt down there you parents let you go to them" says Lisa

"We don't to go to that one we can go to the one in Harlem it's safer at this one" says Rick

"Do you do anything else on Friday nights then fight clubs I just don't feel comfortable going to those places" says Lisa

"That's fine we can do whatever then I am not trying to push you" replies Rick

"I have no more ideas Rick like I said I don't usually go out at night but I want to make you happy if your board lets go and do something" suggests Lisa

"I do like other stuff, I will think of something" says Rick

"Let's go to the Brooklyn wrestling club they have a matches on Friday nights" suggest Rick

"Brooklyn that's too far we will never make it in time" says Lisa

"Right I forgot silly me" laughs Rick

"I am sorry Rick I am not an exciting girlfriend for you" sadly says Lisa

"Your exciting I am having fun just hanging with you" replies Rick

"Are you sure" says Lisa

"Yes I am sure" replies Rick

"I promise I will get better and tomorrow if you're up to it we can go out and have some fun I like arcades" says Lisa

"Now you're talking my language" says Rick

After deciding what they were going to do for the rest of the night, Lisa and Rick got on their and shoes and headed out the door down the stairs of the Tapersty Apartments 245E 124th St standing outside Rick stands at the edge of the sidewalk he sees a taxi coming down the street." Taxi!!" yells Rick, the taxi cab stops and picks up Lisa and Rick the car smelt funny and the driver was a foreigner, he didn't speak good English but he knew where Rick and Lisa were heading when Rick told him, the drive drops Rick and Lisa off at the Pinball arcade located at 362 3rd Ave, Lisa and Rick enter the Arcade this Arcade is open till mid nights on Friday and Saturdays the arcade tonight isn't packed but there are kids playing Lisa and Rick pay then find a games to play.

"This was a good idea" says Rick

"I wanted you to have fun with me tonight since I was so boring" laughs Lisa

Lisa and Rick played the arcade games and stayed for two hours as they were getting ready to leave a voice yells out to Rick

"Hey Ricky" yells Chad

"Hey Chad" replies Rick

"It's fancy seeing you here, and who is this pretty lady that you're hanging with?" asks Chad

"Chad this my girlfriend Lisa Monroe" says Rick

"Lisa good meet you, I was Rick's neighbour we moved to Brooklyn" replies Chad

"Hi Chad nice to meet you" says Lisa

"What the hell man is she shy or something" wonders Rick

"Yes but once you get to know Lisa she's cool to hang with" smiles Rick

"So what are you doing in this neck of the woods I thought you Brooklyn folks were to hi-classed for us common folk" jokes Rick

"My sister got her licence and a car she is grounded for three months, for sneaking out after dark and as punishment she has to drive me anywhere I want to be driven" brags Chad

"That's nice Chad we better be going we had fun were both tired and ready for bed" says Rick

"I am not tired if you're going back to your place then I will get my sister to drive me" says Chad.

"No I am heading to Lisa's place her mom gave us some money to go play the arcade so there are no other visitors allowed" explains Rick

"Hey that's cool who am I to dis respect other people rules" says Chad

Lisa and Rick left the arcade, and got another taxi to take them back to the apartment, when Lisa and Rick got back to the apartment Lisa closed the door and locked it.

"Well that was fun" says Lisa

"Yes it was I enjoyed myself" replies Rick

"Back at the arcade, why did you lie to your friend?" asks Lisa

"Chad is one of those kids he will, make trouble my parents didn't really like him then when his family moved to Brooklyn we lost touch, the family has lots of money and you didn't want him here" explains Rick

"Oh okay I was curious" replies Lisa

"So it's getting late, we should get some shut eye" says Lisa

"Yes I agree with you" replies Rick

"I will go and get some blankets and lets sleep out in the living room tonight on the floor kind of like a camp out" says Lisa

"Not bad I am up for that" replies Rick

Lisa headed down the hall to the linen closet and got out blankets and pillows and gave them to Rick to lie down on the floor, and then she went to her bedroom and put on her night shirt that she had on the night before, once in her shirt, Rick came down the hall carrying his sleepwear.

"Where can I change at Lisa?" ask Rick

"You can use the bathroom to get changed in I have to brush my teeth so I am going to brush my teeth and comb my hair while your changing I promise I won't look" smiles Lisa. Lisa got out her tooth brush and started to brush her teeth Rick was changing and like she promised she didn't look while he was changing until he started to go pee.

"Let me know before you pull that out and pee" smiles Lisa

Lisa was kind of curious so she took a peak looking shocked she looks at Rick and says.

"That is huge man that would tear me apart if we did it I am tiny" says Lisa

"Well were not going to until you're comfortable" says Rick

"I know I was curious that's all I wanted to see what I was in for" flirts Lisa

It was Lisa's turn to go pee she didn't spare anything for Rick she sat down on the toilet and peed, Rick being a boy of course and raging hormones was curious as well, Lisa wasn't wearing any underwear so as she stood up Rick looked at her.

"Were you peaking" says Lisa

"I just peaked for a moment" smiles Rick

"Like what you saw?" asks Lisa in an innocent voice

"Yes I did I only just looked for a second though so I didn't see much" replies Rick

"Well you know what I have now you seen mine I seen yours, let's go to bed and I might let you have a closer peak but just a peak got it" orders Lisa

"Your teasing me aren't you Lisa" says Rick

Laughing out loud Lisa shakes her head yes, laughing together, Lisa and Rick went to bed camped out in the living room with the TV going and a little light shining in and the night time New York breeze blowing into the apartment

The night was a busy down on the path way long the backside of the apartment overlooking the Hudson river, the smell of rain filled the air in the apartment as Rick slept Lisa lays awake wondering how her mom's shift is going, looking at the clock on the wall, that is ticking away tick, tick, tick Lisa looks at the clock and then sighs and gets up from the floor *'2:30 am and I am awake with a boy sleeping next to me on the floor I am going to phone mom and see how her shift at the bar was thought Lisa.*

Lisa calls the Casablanca Hotel Times Square New York City, this hotel the Peggy works at has the bar over on times square close to work, she got the job at the hotel as a front desk agent making not bad money, the Casablanca Hotel is a four star hotel with rooms starting at Thirteen thirty one a night, catering to celebrities and rich travelers

"Casablanca Hotel Times Square Peggy speaking"

"Hi mom, how is your night?" asks Lisa

"Lisa what on earth are you doing awake at 2:35 am in the morning?" asks Mom

"I was just wondering how you were doing that's all missing you right now" says Lisa

"Well you have Rick there with you don't you?" asks Mom

"Yes I do but I still miss you" says Lisa

"Well I miss you too now go back to sleep and I will see you in the morning when I get home" replies Mom

Alone Volume 1

Lisa hangs up with her mom and creeps back to bed and lays down, finally waking up at 7:30 am Lisa gets dressed in some pajama pants, Rick is getting changed in the bathroom once they were changed, Rick and Lisa had breakfast Lisa eating toast and Rick eating cereal.

"How did you sleep last night?" asks Rick

"Fine I was awake at 2:30 this morning but I went back to sleep" replies Lisa

"Was it because I was sleeping next to you on the floor or what?" asks Rick

"No I was missing my mom and wondering how her shift went when she works like this and I am alone I miss her when she works so hard she works three jobs you know

"Why so many?" asks Rick

"She just likes to work that's she had a rough upbringing her mother was a single mother like my mom is and she didn't get the education that she should have gotten so it's hard for her to get a job she got as far as the ninth grade then, she quite school because my grandmother couldn't afford to put her through school so my mom had to get a job" explains Lisa

"Yeah but you're going into the ninth grade so your saying that you might not, be in school anymore next September" says Rick.

"That's why she works so hard is to keep me school, she wants me to have the education that she didn't get" replies Lisa

Just then the door opens and it's Peggy Monroe, looking tired Lisa runs over and gives her mom a hug and a kiss.

"I thought you weren't going to be home until Sunday Mom" says Lisa

"No more night shifts for me at the bar and the hotel, at the bar I got the assistant managers job I applied for and the hotel I got the supervisors position so I am in charge and the best part I don't have to work my clerical job anymore isn't that great" say mom

"That's good news does this mean we can spend Friday nights together too mom?" asks Lisa

"Yes you me and Rick if he wants to or we can have a girl's night one Friday" suggests Mom.

"I like our girls nights" giggles Lisa

"How did you too sleep last night?" asks Mom

"I slept not bad" replies Rick

"After I called you I got back to sleep, and I slept good" says Lisa

"Are you hungry Mom?" asks Lisa

"Yes I am if your cooking breakfast I will eat" replies Mom

Lisa headed to the fridge, she got out three grapefruit, the eggs and the bacon, getting out a pan, and cutting the grapefruit, Lisa gets breakfast as her, mother who has put in a long night shift, changes out of her work clothes and into a pair of sweat pants and a t-shirt, the she joins Lisa in the kitchen to help her, not wanting the help, Lisa tells her mom to sit and she would cook breakfast, Lisa had the coffee on for her mom too, once that was done she poured her mom a coffee and put in two sugar and one cream Lisa takes it over to her mother who is on the couch

"Here you go mom coffee just the way you like it" says Lisa

"Your being a real sweetheart is there something your sucking up for Lisa" says Mom

"No I want to be helpful and give my mommy a coffee" giggles Lisa

"Oh your being silly stop it" laughs mom.

.   **Chapter 6**

Rick thanks for spending the night with Lisa that was mighty nice of you" says Peggy

"You're welcome Lisa is defiantly a kind hearted girl I love spending time with her" replies Rick.

"I am glad that you love, spending time with her you are nice boy and for that I would love for you to hang with Lisa more, when you get the chances to, I am sure your parents have rules for you" says Peggy

"Yes but they do let me do what I want as long as it is within reason though" explains Rick

"So I am not sure what you want to do now Rick that I am home you more than welcome to stay another night if you wish too, or I can drive you home so that you're not taking the bus" offers Peggy, Rick looks at Lisa who is in the kitchen cleaning up Lisa stares back at him and then says.

Alone Volume 1

"If you want to go home I am okay with that, or we can hang some more let mom rest and we can maybe go see a movie" suggest Lisa

"That would be awesome I do want to stay at least one more night, with you and your mom, my sister can be a bore sometimes and very bossy, I better phone her and tell her that I am staying one extra day so she isn't worried about me" says Rick.

"Hello Stephanie" says Rick

"What do you want Rick" snaps Stephanie.

"I am going to stay an extra day at, Lisa's place" explains Rick

"Yeah whatever you little creep" says Stephanie

"She's Okay with me staying an extra night Lisa and Peggy" says Rick

"Great that's great I am going to freshen up and then I am going to join you, guys for a movie if you want or we can just hang and I can get to know Rick" suggests Peggy.

Lisa, Rick and Peggy hung around for the rest of the day this was the happiest that Lisa has been for a while, with her mom and now her boyfriend with her, she has nothing to do be sad about, the three spent the evening playing games and eat pizza, and when it was time for bed, Lisa and Rick slept out in the living room again, mom was in her bed, the night breeze blew in and Lisa could hear the sirens screaming down the road, that was a common occurrence to hear the sirens.

In the morning, Peggy got the kids, breakfast and then Rick was ready to go home, he had a lot of fun hanging with Lisa, and her mom. Lisa and Rick get in the truck and head over to the suburbs of the city Rick's house was nice, it was a red brick house with a big garage and lots of nice grass in the front, Lisa felt kind of ashamed that she was pulling up in this truck in such a nice neighbourhood, but Rick didn't care, sitting in the drive way Rick said his goodbye's Lisa would, see him tomorrow at the funeral for Mrs. Kay Simon Baruch Junior High has been closed since her passing in respect for Mrs. Kay.

On the way home to the apartment Lisa's mom looked at her with a smile and says.

"So Rick seems like he is a very nice guy" says Mom

"Yes he is I really like him" replies Lisa

"Well if you're happy I am happy for you" replies Mom

"You might be happy about this then, Rick has asked me to be his girlfriend" says Lisa

Alone Volume 1

"Wow that is good I accept him being in your life, as long as he doesn't hurt you in any way that will make you hate him, I am good with him dating you and you dating him" explains Mom

"You don't have to worry about that, but what I worry about is why did he choose me I mean I didn't think I could ever love a man, I seen how Scott treated you and I just figured all men were like that" says Lisa

"No honey not all men are like that, Scott was a different animal, I am glad he is out of our lives for good" replies Mom.

Once Lisa and mom got home Lisa cleaned up the living room, from the sleep over and cleaned up the apartment it was nice having her mom home now on the weekends and with Rick in her life, after Lisa was done the chores she headed to her room and laid across her bed and did a journal entry.

Dear Diary:

It's been an interesting few months, I no longer have to deal with the monster in my life, that pain is gone, the scars though will never heal the emotional scars, will be with me, forever Mom and I moved into a place for ourselves I am liking it, there isn't a bucket in the hall way to catch the water when it rains, or there isn't any screaming and shouting and heavy metal music, and the sound of the Harley Davidson Motor Bike that I was, so familiar with. The other day the teacher that liked me and cared so much, for her students passed away, I am going to miss her, we have a new teacher Miss Veronica Appleton, she is very pretty and nice, and so I am going to like her.

Now there is another thing, going on in my life, for the first time in a long time a boy spoke to me, he is a nice boy, his name is Rick Bell same age as me fourteen, at first I thought why is, this boy liking me, but now I realize, why and I have some big news Rick has asked me to be his girlfriend I wasn't sure at first still not sure if, I will make a good girlfriend but I said, yes anyway

Well this is it; I am going to stop writing for now.

After Lisa wrote an entry in her diary, she was called for supper, she and mom had supper then after supper with a little bit of homework left to do, Lisa retired to her room for the rest of the night to finish by the time she was done it would be, time for bed, Lisa finished the English assignment that she was given, with time to spare to say good night to her mom, Lisa left her room and went to mom who was sitting in the living room wrapped up in a blanket and watching TV.

"Good night mom" says Lisa

Alone Volume 1

"Good night sweetie, have a good sleep" replies Mom

Lisa headed to her room and, got changed into a pink night shirt; Lisa pulls back the covers and goes to lay down when the phone in her bedroom rang.

"Hello" answers Lisa

"I just wanted to say, good night and see you at school tomorrow" says Rick

"Same to you, Rick I am just getting ready for bed" flirt's Lisa

"Me too I will think about you tonight as I sleep" says Rick

"That's creepy but sexy" laughs Lisa

After she was done on the phone Lisa set her alarm, and drifted off to sleep, Lisa had her bedroom window open with nice west breeze coming into her room. Lisa heard sirens and heard her mom getting ready for bed she heard the toilet flush and moms door close, Lisa had issues getting to sleep as she was worried about tomorrow the, funeral for Mrs. Kay was in the morning.

Lisa's alarm went off at 6:00 am Lisa got up went pee and had a shower, she went back to her room with a towel around her and went to her closet, to pull out something nice to where, Lisa pulled out a pair of black slacks and a light blue top, heading out to the kitchen Lisa's mom was getting ready to go to work, she had the cereal on the table and the milk, Lisa sat at the table and had her breakfast mom said goodbye to her and she left for work, as soon as she was done breakfast Lisa put things away, grabbed her lunch and headed down stairs to the, lobby and waited for the school bus, the bus arrived and Lisa got on, she spotted Rick she headed down to his seat and sat down.

"Good morning Lisa how are you doing?" asks Rick

"I am good Rick" replies Lisa

The bus took all the students to the school the mood in the bus was that of a somber mood everyone was dressed up nice for the funeral; it was going to be a hard day for most of the students who had Mrs. Betty Kay as their teacher, the bus pulled up in the bus circle of Simon Baruch Junior High, the flags were at half-staff and the school looked different, Rick and Lisa got off the bus as the students and parents and close friends filed into the school gym most of the people holding hands Rick looks at Lisa with a sad somber smile and says.

"Do you mind if I hold your hand and we can walk in together" suggest Rick

"I would like that" replies Lisa

Alone Volume 1

Walking hand in hand into the school, Lisa and Rick were met at the door by a man in a suite handing out memorial cards, Lisa took hers and put it in her pants pocket, Lisa and Rick made their way to the gym and found the seats of Miss Appleton's class now, Miss Appleton spotted Lisa and Rick and sat down beside them, she was wearing a long black dress with a white shirt and a lady's sport coat, Miss Appleton was wiping her eyes with, a tissue she had mascara running down her face, the whole gym was packed and, Mrs. Jones and some other people were up on the stage, Lisa could see the coffin up at the front of the school. Mrs. Jones stood up and made her way to the podium.

"Good day fellow student's teachers, and parents, today is a day of coming together to remember, a wonderful human and a great teacher and an excellent role model. To get this started I am calling up to the podium, Frank Thomas minister of Mrs. Kay" addresses Mrs. Jones.

"Please rise, dearly beloved, we have come together today to mourn the loss of a wonderful lady, Betty Kay was such a wonderful sole that loved to teach and loved kids, as her family is sitting here today, I am reminded how much she loved her family, and how much they loved her, as I have come to know Betty it was apparent to me that she was a special part of the this school.

Betty Kay was born in Brooklyn in 1943, Betty attended school and was a, wonderful student, always wanting to be a teacher Betty graduated and, headed for teachers college, where she met her husband Herb, the two got married and had, three wonderful children together, I was talking to Herb before everyone got here, and he said how wonderful, it was for the school to come together in this time of grief and celebration of life.

I leave you now, with Mrs. Jones once again saying a few words to you all" preaches the minister

"Mrs. Kay will be missed, very much her legacy has been a grand one all though fifty six years of age Betty will be forever in our hearts, I am going to take this time now to invite the students to the cafeteria for a luncheon, of sandwiches and snacks, classes will resume again tomorrow like usual" says Mrs. Jones.

Lisa and Rick headed to the cafeteria for the lunch and the, mingle Lisa had been crying, but she didn't want to show her feelings to Rick that she was sad. The lineup at the cafeteria was long so Lisa and Rick stood in line, there were people still, showing emotions and others acted like they didn't care what happened. Lisa and Rick had their plates in their hands and it was their turn to grab something to eat.

Alone Volume 1

"This line is long I have never seen so many people" says Lisa

"Well Mrs. Kay was popular and she will be missed" replies Rick

"Yes she will be missed, she was the only teacher that really believed in me and my potential" explains Lisa.

"I don't think that is true, you have Miss. Appleton now to, believe in you" says Rick

"Yes she is a good teacher and I like her yes, but you know me I have to take time to trust people that I don't know" says Lisa

While sitting at the table talking Miss. Appleton came over to the table that Rick and Lisa were at with a plate of food, with mascara stains still on her face from crying, she looks at Rick and Lisa with a smile as she says.

"Can I join you, I see no one is sitting here, with you, I think it is sad that no one has" says Miss Appleton.

"By all means Miss Appleton you can join us, Lisa and I we were just going to get seconds or at least I was" laughs Rick

"You go and get seconds I am full and I am staying right here" smiles Lisa

Rick left to go and get some more food, Lisa was still thinking about what, she had said to Rick and how she is starting to trust Miss Appleton, she has only been teaching for three weeks, so far Lisa likes her.

"So Lisa how are you doing today?" asks Miss Appleton

"I am okay, just sad, because of the todays events" replies Lisa

"Yes I know it was a sad day, for everyone" answers Miss Appleton

"You look very pretty today Lisa" compliments Miss Appleton

"Thanks you do too look very pretty" replies Lisa

Rick finally returned with another plate of food he sat down to the left of Lisa and touched her leg, Lisa had the nervous feeling when he did that, but she didn't say anything, Miss Appleton was eating a sandwich and drinking her coffee.

"So Rick you look handsome, today" compliments Miss Appleton

"Thanks you as well Miss Appleton" replies Rick

"So what is the story with you guys?" asks Miss Appleton

"Whatever do you mean" replies Lisa in a confused voice

"What I meant I have seen you guys hanging around together and I was curious if something was going on" wonders Miss Appleton.

"Oh well Miss Appleton, Rick and I became good friends, and were even closer now that he has asked me to be, his girlfriend" brags Lisa

Alone Volume 1

"Well that is charming you guys make a cute couple" says Miss Appleton

"We like to think so" smiles Lisa

After the talking with Miss Appleton and getting to know her, Rick and Lisa grabbed their book bags and headed to the school bus, that was waiting for them, they boarded the bus and sat down, the bus pulled away from the school it wasn't that full of kids so the going home wouldn't take too long.

"Do you want to come to, my place Lisa and meet my mom?" asks Rick

"Okay I have to be home, at 3:00 pm but I guess I can for a bit" replies Lisa

"Cool, my mom wants to meet you" says Rick

"That's nice" says Lisa softly.

Lisa wasn't feeling like meeting anyone today, her anxiety was kicking in and the gears were turning in her head.

The bus stopped off at Ricks house and he and Lisa got off, Lisa walks up the driveway with her legs feeling like jelly and her heart was pounding and her palms were cold and sweaty Lisa and Rick enter the house standing in the front entry way, Lisa took off her shoes and set her bag down, trying to get her legs to keep her up, Lisa struggled to walk, Rick looked back at Lisa and had a concerned look on his face.

"Lisa what is wrong?" asks Rick

"It's an anxiety attack, I get them in upsetting situations that's all they pass with un-stressful situations and meeting your mom is making me anxious" says Lisa

"Well there is really nothing to worry about, you will love my mom" replies Rick

Lisa and Rick headed to the kitchen where Rick hears his mom, moving around.

"Mom I am home" yells Rick

"Hi your home early it's only 12:30" says Mom

"It was Mrs. Kay's funeral today so the school was being used to remember her" explains Rick.

"And you must be Lisa" says Kathy, Lisa smiles at her and trying to find the words to say Lisa got more anxious, to the point where her stomach was hurting.

"Nice to meet you Mrs. Bell" answers Lisa

"We have heard lots about you, Rick can't stop talking about you and he says you are a cutie and, you are" compliments Kathy.

"Thanks, but I think he is just sucking up" laughs Lisa

"A sense of humor I like it" says Kathy

Lisa was starting to sweat and her heart was, pounding more and more, she has had these anxieties attacks before but, this one is a bad one.

"Are you feeling alright Lisa, you're looking a little pale?" asks Kathy

"I will be fine; it's just an anxiety attack, they happen in stressful situations like today and when I meet new people for the first time, they usually pass by now but this one seems to be staying" explains Lisa

"I completely understand, I used to get them when I was your age, so I know what you're going through, but there is nothing to be scared of here, Lisa we don't bite" laughs Kathy.

"I am also extremely shy too, this is not me usually, most of the time I am at home in front of the TV or reading a book, I am kind of loner and I am a real tom boy as well" replies Lisa.

"Well that doesn't matter, it means your unique and that is good, you make Rick happy like I said he can't stop talking about you" repeats Kathy.

"I like Rick too, Mrs. Bell, he has been so good to me, I am really not sure how I am going to repay him for being so kind" explains Lisa

"Well Rick is a good kid, typical teenager but, we have no issue with him, he has a kind heart like his mother and he has his dad's sense of humor, Stan is a good guy just like Rick" says Kathy.

After talking a little bit to Mrs. Bell Lisa's anxiety was getting better the chest pounding had gone away and, the sweaty palms were going away, but the stomach ache was still there, Rick came back from his downstairs bedroom, with a pair of shorts on and a t-shirt, he came back in the kitchen and smiles and Lisa and his mom.

"See what did I tell you, nothing to be afraid of Lisa, my mom is cool" says Rick

"I am feeling better still got gut cramps like they're going to fall out" replies Lisa

Just then Lisa had to get up and use the bathroom she ran to the bathroom as if she was going to be sick, Lisa sat down on the toilet, holding the garbage can, but nothing was coming out of her stomach, she peed a little, but then she got a shock when she went to wipe, there was blood on the tissue, Lisa started shaking again stood up and, came out to the kitchen looking embarrassed

"Lisa you look terrible, what happened?" asked Rick.

Lisa started to cry she turned her, head so not show that she was crying, Rick walks over to put his arm around her, Lisa froze when he did that, so he got his mom, something was defiantly wrong.

"Lisa sweetie are, you okay?" asks Kathy

"No… I have cramps…. And when I went to the bathroom there, was blood in the toilet" cries Lisa.

"Come with me sweetie I know just, what your issue is" says Kathy

Lisa walks with Kathy to, the master bedroom on suite bathroom, and goes into the cupboard below the sink.

"What's wrong with me?" asks Lisa

"Well sweetie, you just had your period" explains Kathy

"Oh my god I feel so embarrassed, I have never had one till now, I am only fourteen" says Lisa.

"Don't be embarrassed Lisa its natural occurrence, for young women your age, I have two girls myself and they went through the same thing as you are going through, here you're going to have to put this in your underwear, this is a period pad its absorbs the blood, you put this on, I am not sure if you want this one or if you want a tampon, the pad might be easier for now" suggests Kathy.

"Okay, so do I have to use it now?" asks Lisa

"Yes if you want I can help you, I had to help my daughters, and they were scared at first" says Kathy.

Lisa moved to the toilet and pulled down her pants and sat on the toilet, she was feeling uncomfortable but she knew that Mrs. Bell was just helping her out, she followed the instructions that Mrs. Bell gave her and once she was done she, stands up, feeling a little bit better Lisa and Kathy head back to the kitchen, where Rick was waiting.

"Everything okay?" asks Rick

"Yes it is Rick, Lisa was just having some girl issues, that is all" explains Kathy

"Well this is, embarrassing I am going to have to go home and change, my clothes, don't be mad at me Rick" says Lisa

"Why would I be mad, I understand I have two sisters, so I know what happens" says Rick

"Thanks for understanding Rick, I do love you and I promise we will hang around more" smiles Lisa

Alone Volume 1

"I love you too Lisa" smiles Rick, Lisa, Rick and Kathy headed to the garage, Katy was going to take Lisa home, but first they had to make a stop at the drugstore, before Lisa could go home, after the stop at the drugstore, Mrs. Bell drove Lisa home, to the apartment.

"I will be right back mom, I am going to take Lisa to her suite" says Rick

"Okay, that's good your being a gentlemen" says Mom

Rick walked up the stairs with Lisa, and waited for her to open the door to the suite; once it was opened Lisa turned to Rick and said.

"Thank you Rick this means a lot to me, you must think that I am dirty and your mom probably thinks I am too" cries Lisa

"No we don't think that, Lisa it happens I still love you regardless" replies Rick

"You're a good boyfriend" says Lisa

Lisa put her arms around Rick and gave him a hug and a kiss on the cheek, Lisa smiles at him and Rick smiles back, as Lisa closes the door, with the drugstore bag in her hand.

Lisa closed the door and slid down, to the floor and started to cry, Lisa sat there for a few minutes trying to wrap her head around what just happened, Lisa sat on the floor by the door, wiping the tears from her eyes, once that was done, Lisa got up and headed to the kitchen for a drink of water, her throat felt dry and, she felt sick to her stomach, then Lisa headed to the mail boxes in the lobby to get the mail, there wasn't much just some junk, and something for her mother, that has Lisa attention, she thought she should open it, but then she didn't it was none of her business and if she wanted to know she would ask her mom.

Taking off her back pack and her shoes, Lisa has a gut ache, bad burning cramps in her stomach same thing she had a Ricks place, she wasn't sure if this was normal or if she should be concerned, the pains went away and, Lisa feels better for a moment then the back ache started again

Same thing she had at Ricks also, Lisa went back to the kitchen and she took another drink of water, this time she wasn't feeling good again and she wanted to puke, with butterflies in her stomach Lisa sat on the floor hoping she would feel better, once she started to feel better she didn't want to move much, the pain seems to stop when she doesn't move, *'This isn't any good, every time I move I seem to get cramps or I feel like I am going puke, what is going on could also be something else is the reason I feel sick' though Lisa*

Alone Volume 1

Lisa stood back up again and she got the same doubling pain that has hit her three times now, this time she is really concerned, the food she ate at the school tasted funny, maybe it was food poisoning, tabled with her period on top of that, slowly moving to the kitchen again Lisa takes another drink of, water only to have the garbage can beside her to vomit, Lisa felt sick and helpless, she had never felt like this before and she was scared, now that she was in the apartment if she could make it to her bed room she would, change and make something for her sick stomach .

Chapter 7

Once Lisa was inside the apartment, she headed to her bedroom looking for a change of pants and underwear, she found some grey leggings that she settled for, Lisa then headed for the shower, she felt dirty and she wanted to clean, herself once she was clean and had a new pad on, Lisa headed out to the living room, to watch TV. She still felt ashamed and wondered what Rick and his mother thought, this happened to an embarrassing moment for Lisa that she doesn't want to remember with the TV going and laying down on the couch Lisa's mother walks in from work.

"Lisa I am home" calls mom

"Hi mom" says Lisa

"How was your day?" asks Lisa

"It was good, it's nice to be home although didn't you have school today?" asks Mom

"It was the funeral for Mrs. Kay and it was a half day" replies Lisa

"Did you hang with Rick at all today?" asks

"Yes I did I had kind of an embarrassing moment, we went to his place his mom wanted to meet me" says Lisa

"Well that shouldn't be an embarrassing moment for you" says Mom

"It wasn't embarrassing meeting her it's what happened I feel embarrassed about" says Lisa

"What happened?" asks Mom

"I had my first period, Mom I felt embarrassed because I didn't expect it to happen, so soon Rick's mother was nice enough to help me, out and make me feel better I thought it was just my anxiety due to the events of the morning" explains Lisa

"That would be embarrassing, but it happens honey you need not to be embarrassed its natural for us women to have them, sometimes they happen at the worst possible time" says mom

"And that was the worst time for me" replies Lisa

Alone Volume 1

"Well we are going over there to thank Rick's Mom" says Mom

"I did already she bought me the stuff to wear" says Lisa

"Well we are heading there to see how much we owe her I like that she was so nice to you, but I don't want people thinking that we are a charity case" explains Mom

Lisa and her mom headed outside to the old truck and they took off for Rick's place, once arriving there, Lisa and her mom got out of the truck and went to the front door, and rang the bell Rick answered.

"Mrs. Monroe and Lisa hi" says Rick

"Hi Rick how are you" smiles Peggy

"Good I am really good" says Rick

"That's good, is your mom home?" asks Peggy

"Where are my manners come in and she will be right there" replies Rick, Lisa and her mom entered the big house both women waited in the living room, for Mrs. Bell to come out of the kitchen.

"You must be Mrs. Bell" says Peggy

"Peggy Monroe Lisa's Mom" introduces Peggy.

"Nice to meet you Mrs. Monroe, would you like a coffee or a tea" offers Mrs. Bell

"Sure I will have a coffee" replies Peggy

"Why don't you come to the kitchen and we will have our coffee" says Mrs. Bell

"So what brings you by?" asks Mrs. Bell

"Well I had to meet you first off second I have to thank you for helping Lisa through her embarrassing moment today, It makes me feel good that, there is caring people that will help out" says Peggy.

"Not to worry Peggy, I have two girls myself and besides I am a nurse at the hospital so it was no big deal to help out Lisa" explains Mrs. Bell

Peggy reaches into her purse while Mrs. Bell was getting the coffee; Peggy had some money for Mrs. Bell to pay her for Lisa's feminine products, when the coffee was brought to the table Mrs. Bell sits down and Peggy hands her twenty five dollars, Mrs. Bell looked confused she looks and says

"What's this for Peggy?" asks Mrs. Bell

"I am paying you back for Lisa's feminine products that you bought for her earlier today it's much appreciated" says Peggy

"You don't have to pay me back this, I was just being kind and there is no payment required, besides if anyone owes anybody it's me for having Rick at your home and hanging with your beautiful daughter, so I think we are even in that sense" explains Mrs. Bell

"It was no problem now that I am home on the weekends now, I can spend the time with her" explains Peggy.

"Well Lisa is welcome here anytime she wants, to come and see Rick and meet the rest of the family" says Mrs. Bell

"Thank you this is a lovely home you got here" replies Peggy

"Thanks we bought it to raise our family" says Kathy

"What are you and Lisa doing on Friday, if you're not doing anything I would like to have you and her over for supper to meet the rest of the family my girls and my husband" offers Kathy

"I don't have any plans on Friday we were just going to maybe order Chinese food and watch a movie, but supper sounds great, what time on Friday?" asks Peggy

"Supper is at 6:00 so come around 4:30 or 5:00 pm should be good" answers Kathy

Once Lisa and her mom were finished visiting they headed out to the, truck Rick came out with them.

"See you in school tomorrow Lisa" says Rick

"Yes see you too hopefully" laughs Lisa

Lisa and her mom headed home it was going on New York rush hour, so Peggy wanted to get home before she got stuck in traffic, she pushed the pedal to the old truck, the sputtered and back fired then just before Lisa and her mom get home the truck, quits running.

"No don't quite now, you fucking peace of shit truck" yells Peggy, Peggy got the truck started again and they limped home with the truck, wanting to die, when Lisa and her mom pulled up to the spot, the truck died again this time they were parked, Peggy tries it again and nothing happened.

"Well it looks like I am going to have to call Steve again, to come and pick this thing up, not sure how I am going to get to work tomorrow now that the truck its broken" says mom

Lisa and Peggy headed up to the apartment, Peggy called Steve's auto repair the mechanic she has gone to for years with the truck, when she was done Lisa and her mom had a quick bite to eat and they met Steve out at the front of the apartment building the big tow truck pulled up, and Steve got out, Steve Green has been a friend of Peggy for years, Steve is bigger guy tall in height, divorced middle aged man, but a sweet man who has always, managed to give Peggy a break.

"Hey ladies how are you" says Steve

Alone Volume 1

"Were good Steve" replies Peggy

"Lisa you have grown in to a beautiful girl just like your mother here" compliments Steve

"So let's have a look at the truck hop into mine I will hook up and we will go to my, shop and see what the issue is" says Steve

Steve took the old 1987 Chevy Truck to his shop, he fixes cars and he also sells used cars Peggy gets out of the tow truck with Lisa, the two walked around the car yard looking at the vehicles, about twenty minutes later Steve comes back wiping his hands and wiping his forehead.

"I am afraid Peggy I can't fix the truck, she dead, you have a major oil leak on the manifold and your transmission is ready to go, you need front end work brakes, ball joints wheel baring's going to cost more to fix it then what the truck worth" explains Steve

"Well I knew the time would come, that I would have to replace the old beast, so I guess I will have to pick one of these vehicles that you have here" says Peggy

"Wow your buying from me" jokes Steve

"Yes Steve I am, I need something more reliable, how about that Blue truck over there that Ford F150" says Peggy

"Well that one isn't a bad truck everything works has power windows low miles on it only eighty five thousand miles on it" says Steve

"How much for it Steve and give me a good number" orders Peggy

"Well I am asking seventy five hundred for it, but since you have been so good of a customer the lowest I can go, and still a profit is forty five hundred" says Steve

"Forty five hundred hey, well what can you give me for my old truck I need some money down I will have make payments to you if that is okay Steve" says Peggy

"You can make payments, I normally would give money for vehicles that I am not going to make a profit off of, but since you're need of a vehicle, I will make you a deal" says Steve

"That sounds good, what is the offer?" asks Peggy

"Eleven hundred dollars for your, old truck today, that goes towards the new one that your, getting then the rest of it in payments, of whatever you, can give me I am flexible especially with you, since were such good friends" says Steve.

"I can do that, I need vehicle" replies Peggy.

"Great I will go and get the keys to this one and gas it up for you, then you can do what you need for your old truck" says Steve

Alone Volume 1

Peggy and Lisa headed to the garage and started to clean out the, old truck there wasn't much in it, but the stuff that was in it was important, Lisa grabs a screwdriver and takes off the licence plate off of the old truck, Peggy could see Steve heading back from gassing up the, truck, Steve drives it to bay 1 where Peggy and Lisa are standing waiting, Steve gets out of the truck grabs the plate from Lisa, as the ladies headed to the new truck, Peggy gets in and she looks at her new purchase, once Steve is done putting the plate on, he comes to the front door of the truck.

"There you be ladies, enjoy this ride" says Steve

"How much do I owe you, for the tow?" asks Peggy?

"Nothing have, me over, one night for some of the amazing roast beef and Lisa's wonderful fudge brownies" says Steve

"Sounds good" laughs Peggy.

Lisa and her mom head home in their brand new wheels the drive, home was quite Lisa wasn't feeling well yet, after her moment at Rick's place, once Lisa and her mom were home, Lisa heads for the shower, to clean up, then Lisa put on some pajama's and went to bed, the night was long and Lisa was still not feeling well she had anxiety attacks before but never involving anything like the moment that she experienced, Lisa lays awake staring off into space, the window to her room is open and the door is closed and locked, Lisa rolls over and looks at the clock, Midnight it read, so Lisa turned on her lamp and started to read a book maybe that would help her sleep a bit

After an hour or so of reading, Lisa was still not feeling well the stomach cramps were unbearable and it felt like someone was punching her in the stomach, then Lisa got up and headed out to the kitchen for a glass of apple juice maybe that would calm her stomach and she can sleep sounder after all she has school in the morning, Lisa downs the apple juice and starts back to bed, but before she could go back to bed, her stomach began to turn, and she felt sick to her stomach, running to the bathroom Lisa turns on the tap to the sink then kneels down on the floor by the toilet to throw up, when Lisa was done, she got up and headed back to bed, she felt like she was going to die and she was warm to the touch Lisa, went to her room and sat on the edge of the bed breathing and trying to get rid of, the hiccups, she looks at the clock and it was 1:30 am in four and a half hours she would get up for school, Lisa lays back down curls up in a ball and tries to get some, sleep, she must of slept well she had heard her mom get, up so she got up herself, and headed out to the kitchen feeling all light sensitive Lisa's mom looked at her then she ran over to Lisa and puts her. Hand on her head and says.

"Oh my god girl you are burning up, I can't send you to school like that" you're going to have to stay home for the day, why don't you call Rick and ask him to bring you some homework home" suggest mom.

Lisa went to the phone to call rick she was sick she had trouble dialing the phone her fingers were weak and her whole body ached like she had been hit by a freight train.

In a raspy voice Lisa talks to Rick and asks him to bring, her some homework, he was happy to do that, after all Rick is her boyfriend, Lisa saw her mom off to work, then grabbed the blanket and pillow off of her bed and put it on the couch, TV was going to be her best friend today, Lisa laid in front of the TV trying to feel better by mid-afternoon after have some chicken noodle soup that Lisa had cooked for herself, and some ginger ale Lisa was starting to feel better, at exactly 3:30 pm the buzzer rings she heads to the key pad to see, who it is, it was Rick, Lisa unlocked the door so that Rick could come in.

"Hi how are you feeling?" asks Rick

"A little better, not much better" replies Lisa

"I have your homework, for you its easy Math and that was it you didn't miss much" says Rick

"Oh I thought I would have missed lots, after all it is a regular day of school" says Lisa

"Some of the classes were still grieving" explains Rick

"I will get this done and I will be back tomorrow at school" says Lisa

"Okay I missed you today" replies Rick

"I missed you as well but I didn't feel well so I didn't come to school" explains Lisa

"I got to go my mom is waiting for me outside she says to feel better" says Rick

"Okay I will see you tomorrow and see you on Friday for dinner as well" replies Lisa

Rick left the apartment, and Lisa shut the door and headed to her room to do her math homework she was good in math and all the other subjects, Lisa laid across her bed, and started the pages assigned, after losing of time, Lisa headed out to the kitchen, to cook some supper the door was just opening, and her mom walks in with some groceries and looking tired her mom turns to look at Lisa as she is standing in the kitchen in her pajama's and uncombed hair.

"You're supposed to be lying in bed and starting to feel better young lady" says mom

"I was feeling better, so I wanted to get the supper done" replies Lisa

"You're still supposed to be resting, but since your up and cooking I will go and have a shower, and get into my pj's" says mom

Lisa cooked supper while her mom was showering and she put the groceries away that her mom had brought home from the supermarket, then Lisa seen a envelope with the DMV address on it, it was the truck registration Lisa left that alone, and went through the rest of the mail, she noticed there was a letter from the school, in the pile of mail, she got a lump in her throat and felt like she was going to be sick, again just then her mom came out to the kitchen from the shower, mom grabbed the mail and headed to the kitchen table, Lisa went about cooking supper, she was hoping that the letter from the school wasn't anything bad.

Mom was sitting at the table and reading the mail Lisa noticed out of the corner of her eye that the next thing she was opening was the thing from the school, Lisa felt sick again to her stomach, she watched as her mom opened the, envelope, Lisa was fixated on her mom for a moment she seen her facial expressions change as she kept reading, then mom got up and went to the stove and stood beside Lisa.

"That was your report card, not bad, some low grades but nothing that I am going to yell at you for, but Miss Appleton wants to talk to me, do you know what that is all about Lisa" explains Mom.

"No I don't maybe it's just say how good of student that I am and she wants to meet you after all she is my new teacher now" replies Lisa.

"So I am going to pick you, up from school and I am going to meet, Miss Appleton" orders mom

"Okay" says Lisa, with supper done cooking Lisa headed to get the plates and stuff to set the table, Lisa wondered what Miss Appleton wanted to see mom about after all Lisa just keeps to herself and does what she is supposed to at school, she doesn't understand why that Miss Appleton would be requesting to see mom, during supper Lisa and her mom chatted about girl things, that only seems to be what they talk about, now that things are going good and mom is home, more Lisa will talk about the things that are bothering her, after supper was done Lisa put all the dishes in the dishwasher then headed to her room to finish her math homework.

Alone Volume 1

Still not feeling well, Lisa headed to the bathroom to have, a nice warm bath with some bubbles that was her favorite and in this place she can have the bubble bath the bath room doesn't leak in this place, after her bath Lisa headed to be to get some more sleep, she crawled into bed with a fresh pair of pajama's and went to sleep, Lisa's alarm went off, and it was time to get up for school, feeling much better Lisa headed to the bathroom and did what she had to do, then went to her room and picked out what she was going to wear for school, mom had already left for work, so Lisa went into her drawer and got out a pair of black leggings and pulled out a blue skirt with a pink top to with it, then she decided not to have her pony tail in she just left her hair hang down.

Lisa grabbed pop tarts and headed out the door for the, bus when the bus came she board the bus Rick was sitting in the usual seat, and rode with him, to the school.

"Hi Lisa" says Rick

"Hi Rick" answers Lisa

"I see you're feeling better" says Rick

"Yes much better then yesterday" says Lisa

"You're looking stunning today wearing a skirt and leggings and wearing your hair down, this look suites you as well, brings out the color in your eyes more" compliments Rick.

"Thanks I did it for you too silly, I wanted you to notice me" says Lisa

"I do notice you, and I said you're very pretty" says Rick

The bus got to the school and Lisa and Rick got off the bus, and walked into the school together, since Lisa and Rick have been together she hasn't been bullied by Jason the bully, dating Rick seems to do the trick, Lisa and Rick were the second ones in class, Miss Appleton was already sitting at her desk, she looks up from her desk from, the papers that she was, looking at and smiles at Lisa.

"Hi Lisa nice to see you, how are you feeling?" asks Miss Appleton

"I am feeling good, I got my math homework for you, too" says Lisa

Lisa got up from her desk and gave Miss. Appleton the math homework, Miss Appleton took it and smiles at Lisa, Lisa heads back to her desk that suddenly seemed closer to Rick's desk, Lisa sat down and got her books, out as the other kids came in for the day.

"Good morning class" says Miss Appleton

"Good morning Miss Appleton" replies the class

Alone Volume 1

"Nice to see everyone here, I hope you all got your report cards some of you, I was impressed with, others not so much, now I am meeting with parents to, introduce myself if you were wondering why I am wanting a meeting, I figure since I am teaching everyone for the rest of the year and hopefully next year in the 9th grade, I figure I should get to know everyone better" explains Miss Appleton.

Lisa felt better knowing why Miss Appleton wanted to see, her mom it wasn't anything serious, Miss Appleton started to teach, something that Lisa had seen much, of since Mrs. Kay got sick and died, it's just been free study with no structured lesson today there was and it was a fun day for Lisa, the lunch bell rang and the students couldn't believe that the morning had gone so fast, Lisa closed her books and headed out to for lunch, Rick came out behind her.

"So did you bring lunch or would, you like some cafeteria food" suggests Rick

"I brought lunch after being sick, I don't trust the food here yet, I don't think that is what made me sick, but I am not chancing it, but you can have lunch here I don't mind" says Lisa

"Okay you might as well hang with me in line, to make sure I make a healthy choice" jokes Rick.

'I am not your, mother" laughs Lisa, Lisa and Rick ate lunch together, it had been two months since they had met, and Lisa was getting used to Rick, hanging around, still insecure though about what could, happen Lisa plays her cards close to her, chest, when the lunch bell rang, Lisa and Rick headed back to class to get through the rest of the afternoon Rick's mother was coming in, to see Miss Appleton as well.

Back in class Miss Appleton had the video machine out, and as promised the class was getting a video assignment to write about, after it was done, as soon as the all the class was in, Miss Appleton, closed the door and ran the video player she turned out one set of lights and closed the blinds, then sat down at her, desk as the video played, most of the afternoon was spent working on this assignment in social studies, when the video was over, Miss Appleton turned the lights back on and opened the blinds and began a class discussion until the bell rang, to signal the end of the day. The kids whose parents weren't here yet, got to home, but Rick and Lisa's mom were waiting to see Miss Appleton, Lisa and her mom were first, to meet with Miss Appleton, Lisa's mom followed Lisa into the class as Miss Appleton called them in.

Alone Volume 1

"You must be Peggy Monroe, it is nice to meet you, I am Veronica Appleton" says Miss Appleton.

"Nice to meet you" says Peggy.

"Now as I explained to the students this morning, I want to meet everyone, especially you Miss Monroe, and I will tell you why" says Miss Appleton

"Lisa is a very brilliant student I can tell she likes school and works hard on her homework, but I sensed something, with the first assignment that I gave to the class it was a writing assignment, to explain how the class felt about different things in life, well Lisa hands back a three page thing I wasn't expecting to read, she indicated that, the monster in her life is gone what does she mean?" asks Miss Appleton

"Well I think what she meant was my ex, see when Lisa was real young, her dad the real dad committed suicide, after taking an acid trip, times were different, well I met this man who I thought, at the time was sweet, then he turned into a real jerk, he wasn't nice too Lisa I just feared for her when she was alone with him, I know he didn't do anything to harm her, but I feared, well I just got out of the relationship and were getting things back on track, so that is what I believe she meant by that" explains Peggy.

"That would make sense other than that, I like teaching Lisa and her and Rick Bell are a real item too" laughs Miss Appleton.

"Yes they are, he's a good kid he's good for Lisa to have someone like that in her life" says Peggy, "I agree we do" says Miss Appleton. Miss Appleton said goodbye to Lisa and her mom as they left the class room Peggy says good bye to Ricks mom who was sitting with Rick in the hall two women have become good, friends since they met, on the way home Peggy looks at Lisa

"So she seems nice" says Mom

"Yeah she is I really like her" replies Lisa

"So I was right to explain what I did in the class, room was Scott really the monster in your life Lisa" wonders mom

"Yes he was, I was really scared of him, and he didn't do anything to hurt me when you weren't home, he was just verbally abusive and threatened to touch me in places, he never did" explains Lisa.

"Good because if I found out that he hurt my little girl I would kill" says mom

The trip home in rush hour was long, Lisa and her mom were getting hungry so they stopped at Peggy Sue's dinner for a burger and fries, as they went in and ordered and waited for food, the person she didn't want to see, walks in to the dinner with his buddies, she tried to look invisible but Scott had spotted her.

"Hello Peggy" says Scott

"What do you want" snarls Peggy

"Just wanted to say, hi and talk that's all" says Scott

"Well hi now would you please go to hell and leave us alone" demands Peggy

"Fine then I just thought that maybe you would consider taking me, back but I guess you're not ready, I understand and I will see you again I hang out here most times I am a changed man now, I wanted you to see that" says Scott

"That's good, I am not ready to talk to you okay when I am ready I will speak to you" explains Peggy

The food came and Lisa and her mom ate fast to get out of the restaurant in fact they took their food home, to eat it.

Running to the new truck as fast as they could, not wanting Scott to go after them Peggy speeds off, before heading home. Lisa and her mom had to go stop at the supermarket, for some groceries. Peggy and Lisa moved fast so not to let their supper get cold.

"So do you, believe that he has changed, mom?" asks Lisa

"I don't know sweetie, I am not wanting to think about it at all, I just want to think about you and I" replies mom

"Well I don't want him back in our lives, have you thought about Steve as a man for you, I mean you have known him for a long time, and I like him" says Lisa

"Steve is only a friend but there might be a chance that we could, get together" hints mom

Lisa and her mother move in a fast pace in the grocery store, as they head to the check out to pay for the food, once the food was paid for Lisa and her mom got back to the truck, and headed home to the apartment,

on their way through Peggy made one more stop before heading home the stop was to another store again, this time Lisa went in with her mom, but she was feeling hungry and was sluggish on the walk around this store, once Peggy Monroe got what she had to get, Lisa and Peggy headed back to the apartment.

Alone Volume 1

Chapter 8

With food in hand and arriving at the apartment, Lisa and Peggy closed the door and locked it all up and closed, the blinds to be sure that they weren't followed home, with their hearts pounding and palms sweaty, Lisa and Peggy sit down at the table to eat their food and drink their milkshakes

"That is the last person I wanted to see, he'd better not come around here" says Peggy

"I hope he doesn't either, I don't want to see him" replies Lisa

"If he decides to come and bug you at school, just have Mrs. Jones call the police" warns mom, "Ricks dad is a cop so I can get Rick to call his dad, but Scott wouldn't dare come around to the school with his gang, to many kids around" says Lisa

"Don't be too sure, if he knows that were doing well for ourselves then, he is liable to come and try to come back" says Peggy

"Mom did you really use your 401k to pay for this place, I believe that you worked hard to get this for us, but I know that you wouldn't cash that in" says Lisa

"Well if you want to know the truth honey, I went through affordable housing, to get this place we, get a reduced rate for rent, and this was the only way we, could get out of the shit hole we were living in" explains Mom.

"You know I love you mom you're a strong women and you can handle anything, but I do worry that the pressures of, hiding and living your life in fear of evil, will take its toll on a person" says Lisa.

"You have a good, point honey and I am trying to make things right, now seeing Scott makes me wonder if he is going to track us down, and lord knows what, he would do" warns Mom

"I know you're making things, right and I am happy with the way that life is going right now and I don't want anything to change" says Lisa

"I don't want anything to, change either, I am glad we parked out of sight so if, Scott does come by, he won't suspect that I have new wheels I don't think he even looked when we, left" replies mom.

Lisa finished her burger and fries and her milkshake, with a simple dinner, Lisa and her mom spent the rest of the night looking through the Sears book looking for summer wear.

Alone Volume 1

"So my new boss at my job, has offered us his summer home, up in Great Falls, I was thinking that at some point we, can go there when school lets out, and you can ask Rick if he wants to come" suggests Mom

"That would be nice we could certainly use a break especially you mother you work so hard to put the roof over our heads and to keep the food on the table" compliments Lisa

"Yes I do need, it and your right, but I still love you Lisa and that will never change" says mom. After giving her mom and hug and a kiss, Lisa headed to bed to get ready for school in the morning, Lisa put on her pajama's put her dirty close in the laundry hamper and climbed into bed and set her alarm.

The night's sleep was long Lisa tossed and turned seeing Scott's face and she was wondering what would happen now that he has seen, that her and mom are happy, Lisa shuttered to think of what could happen, in the morning when her alarm went off she got up, and got ready for school as mom was cooking bacon and eggs and toast for breakfast, Lisa emerged from her room.

"Good morning honey, how did you sleep?" asks Mom

"Okay I didn't sleep the best; I thought too much last night" replies Lisa

"Try not to worry too much I will look after things" says Mom

Lisa ate her breakfast that her mom cooked for her Lisa had on a pink top with grey leggings and her hair was in a ponytail.

"Lisa honey those leggings look good on you but are that all you're going to wear, it's kind of reveling" says Mom

"I like them and I have garments on" explains Lisa

"Just concerned that's all" replies mom

Lisa and her mom headed downstairs together, Lisa to the bus and Peggy to the truck, Lisa's mom gave her a kiss as the bus pulled up, Lisa got on and headed to the seat where Rick was sitting, Lisa waved at her mom as the bus pulled away, Rick was looking out the window as the bus drove down the street he turns to Lisa and says

"How are you doing today Lisa?" asks Rick

"I am doing fine Rick" replies Lisa

"You're looking fine today" flirt's Rick

"Thanks" responds Lisa

The bus pulls up to the school and the kids get off the bus, Lisa and Rick were the last ones off the bus this morning, standing on the curb as the bus pulls away, Lisa notices a black van sitting in the school parking lot she

Alone Volume 1

had never seen it before, and it looked kind of creepy then she spotted a figure of a man sitting in the van.

"Let's go inside I am ready" says Lisa anxiously

"What's wrong, you look like you have seen a ghost" says Rick

"It's nothing I just need to get inside the school with you, and then I will be safe" replies Lisa

"Lisa there is something wrong, you are spooked about something, I spotted a black van with a person sitting in it was like the guy was watching me" explains Lisa

"Oh well I am here to protect you" comforts Rick

"Thanks you're a good friend and boyfriend" smiles Lisa

Lisa and Rick entered the class room, the other kids were in the room they were the last ones to enter the class, they took their seats and Miss. Appleton started to teach, as she was teaching Lisa got a chill down her spine, then the class room phone rang, it was Mrs. Jones asking for Lisa, Miss Appleton goes over to Lisa, and says

"That was Mrs. Jones you need to go to the office" says Miss. Appleton

"Okay did she say what it was about" replies Lisa

"No dear she didn't" expresses Miss Appleton

Lisa got up and grabbed her bag, and left the class room with her bag over her shoulder she noticed the black van still sitting there, she got spooked again and started walking fast to the office, once there Mrs. Jones was waiting for her.

"Good morning Lisa" says Mrs. Jones

"Hi" replies Lisa

"I have called you down here, because your mother has phoned the school to say that she forgot that you have a dentist appointment, this morning she says you should be able to go down by yourself and she will pick you, up from the office if you just call her" explains Mrs. Jones

"Okay I will go now" says Lisa

Lisa leaves the office and heads out the front doors she knows how to get to the dentist office, walking briskly, Lisa spots the black van following her, feeling freaked out, Lisa took a turn down the alley close to the dental office, Lisa runs down the alley way toward the door of the dental office, Lisa enters Dr. Amy Lights office, Lisa checks in with the receptionist breathing rapidly, Lisa sits down and waits for her name to be called feeling safe in the office, Lisa relaxes, Lisa is called into the office to see the dentist, she waited for the dentist to give her the report, after

79

Alone Volume 1

receiving a good report, Lisa heads out feeling confident that, she could be safe to walk back to school, Lisa starts out feeling proud that she got a good report, Lisa took the same alley the way she went, when she was being followed by the van, suddenly three big guys emerge from the alley, these men were all tattooed up with big bellies and wearing black leather.

Lisa screams but her screams went ignored, the three men had grabbed her, knocked out, Lisa could feel the motion of a vehicle, finally when she awoke she woke up in a little room with a mattress on the floor, and bucket beside it, the room was dark and there was only a little light, from a barred window, scared to death, not knowing where she is Lisa sat in the corner, with her knees to her chest, and rocked back and forth with tears in her eyes the nightmare that she lived, has come back to her, she heard voices and seen boots at the, door frightened, Lisa starting praying that, nothing would happen to her.

The door opens and in walks a man standing almost seven feet tall tattooed up, with a beard he looks at Lisa and with a gruff voice says to her,

"You're a wake little girl" laughs the man

Lisa could smell the scent of beer on him and his heavy breathing as he steps closer to her, suddenly it went dark again, and when Lisa awoke she was, sitting tied to a chair, with a light shining down her, then the same voice, says

"You're here we have been following you, I am sure that you know who we are but if you're scared, to look at us, well then we are your worst nightmare" says the voice

Lisa looks at the, guy sitting on the chair in front of her, she could make out a figure, and the figure was sitting backward on the chair, laughing, smiling and breathing heavy, Lisa feeling scared, peed and pooped her pants.

"You didn't you sick girl, you pissed and shit yourself, what are you two years old" says the man

Not saying nothing Lisa, hears the sound of a motorbike pulling up the figure, gets up and goes to the door, Lisa could here vaguely "I have the girl, but she has messed herself" replies the voice, finally all lights come on and standing in front of her is Scott.

"Lisa how good to see you again, I missed you" says Scott.

"Why... are... you... doing... this" stutters Lisa

"You know I don't like doing these things, but you disrespected me last night, you know what happens, when people disrespect us, they pay, but

Alone Volume 1

I am going to not harm you if you tell, me where your living at, and why you moved.

Lisa looks Scott in the face, and says to him.

"You will have to hurt me or kill me before you will know where, mom and I moved too" yells Lisa

"Now, now I don't want to, but if that is what you want then that is what you will get, and I don't want to mess up the pretty little face, of yours" says Scott

Lisa was still shaking and she, was sitting in her own mess, the more she got scared, the more she peed and let her bowels go, Lisa prayed that they would let her go, with a headache from being hit in the head, Lisa prays that help will come, after all day of sitting in her own mess, and feeling really scared the bikers sat around playing cards, and drinking beer she could see Scott out of the corner of her eye, her glasses were missing and her shirt was torn, Lisa sobbed to herself and thought about her mother, Oh she must be frantic looking for her, with not returning to school.

5:00pm Tuesday May 4th 1999

The phone rang as Peggy Monroe franticly worried about Lisa, who had not returned to school, not knowing where she was, Peggy headed over to the Bells, house hoping that Rick had seen her.

"Rick oh my god is Lisa here" cries Peggy

"NO!!! I haven't seen her since this morning she was called to the office, she grabbed her bag and I was hoping she would comeback she never did" explains Rick.

"Oh my god my baby, she is gone, I am such a bad mother" cries Peggy

"We will find her, Peggy" says Mrs. Bell

Rick Peggy and Kathy headed out in search of Lisa, Peggy traced her steps from the school, she always took an alley way, to the dentist office, Kathy turned down the, alley and Peggy got out and started searching, suddenly she sees a back pack, she grabs the bag and franticly runs back to the Kathy's SUV.

"This is Lisa's my god she has gone missing" yells Peggy

"I am going to call the police and get my husband on this for you; he is one of New York's best cops if anyone can find Lisa, it's him" says Kathy

Kathy calls the NYPD and her husband's detachment; she gave a description of what Lisa was wearing, and what she looked like, then Rick noticed something else on the ground, he jumps out of the SUV and picks up a pair of eye glasses, still intact.

"These are Lisa's she was hear" says Rick

"The police are searching, let's go back to my place and fix you a coffee and I think you better stay the night at our place" suggests Kathy

6:00pm Tuesday May 4th at the Lucky bikers club house thirty-five miles west of the city

"So are you ready to talk yet, or do we have to do something, to you" replies Scott

"Like I said, you will have to kill me, or beat me, before I will say anything to you, you rotten piece of shit" snarls Lisa

"Really is that kind of talk, called for, you are kind of my kid I can see that, your mother hasn't taught you, any respect I think I need to teach you some" warns Scott

"Bite me" yells Lisa

Scott getting mad gets up and walks up to Lisa and grabs her by the hair and tips her head back, another biker held a six inch switchblade knife to her throat.

"Now you tell, what I want to know, or the contents of your throat will be on this knife" warns the biker

Again Lisa peed herself and released her bowels for the fourth time of doing that, and sitting in her own mess, finally after two hours of scaring her and threatening, Scott gets a guilty feeling

"Let her go, guys she will not talk to me, and she is my daughter" says Scott

Finally after her terrifying ordeal, the bikers let Lisa go, missing her glasses Lisa walks out into the night, dazed and confused, and hurting from being held against her will Lisa started walking she could see the city lights, Lisa walked toward the lights, with light rain and the sound of wildlife, doing their evening call, Lisa walks hungry tired and dirty.

11:30pm Tuesday May 4th 1999, six hours since fourteen year old Lisa Monroe, was picked up, by Scott's biker buddies, Peggy sits up in the living room of the Bell residence Katy sleeping on the couch and Rick sleeping on the floor, Peggy gets up, and goes to make herself a cup of coffee to relax, Stan walked into the house and, seen Peggy sitting up.

"We have had all kinds of leads in Lisa's disappearance, we believe that she was abducted, is there anyone at all that would have a grudge against you, to do this?" asks Stan

"No I don't we keep to ourselves, most of the time" answers Peggy

Alone Volume 1

Rick had heard his dad, ask the question Rick gets up and goes into the kitchen and says

"This morning when we went to school, she had seen a mysterious black, van sitting in the parking lot, she looked scared, she thought that, the person in the van was watching her" explains Rick.

"Thanks son that helps" says Stan

"We have the helicopter out looking for her, now" replies Stan

Walking in the field with the club house still in sight and the city seeming like it was a million miles away, Lisa passes out, from hunger, all of sudden the NYPD chopper hovers over the field the men on board discover Lisa laying there, they radio in to all other units, and take her to the nearest hospital, Lisa was in terrible looking condition pale, and very clammy with a low heartbeat, Lisa was flown to the New York Metropolitan Hospital.

Wednesday May 5th 1999 2:30 am, the phone of Constable Stan Bell rang, Stan picked it up and it was one of his fellow officers letting him know that Lisa was found but, she wasn't in good shape.

"They found Lisa, she has been taken to the Metropolitan Hospital, I must tell you they say she is in bad condition" replies Constable Bell

Peggy, Rick and Kathy jumped up and headed to Peggy's truck with constable bell leading them in the curser, arriving at the hospital met by the other police officers Peggy runs toward the doors, the officers stop her and calm her down,

"She is safe and sound the doctor is waiting for you Miss. Monroe

Peggy went into the hospital accompanied by Rick, Kathy and Stan, they head toward the nurses station, the nurse at the desk, a black women asks Peggy if she can be helped.

"Can I help you man?" asks the nurse

"I am here to see my daughter was brought in tonight" explains Peggy

"I will the doctor" replies the nurse.

"Hi I am Doctor Andrew Conrad, you must be Miss Monroe" inquires the doctor

"Yes I am, how is my daughter?" asks Peggy

"I am not going to sugar coat it, but she is in very rough condition, we had to stabilize her and wrap her head, with bandages, she has been sent to x ray we believe whoever did this to her, hit her twice with a blunt object in the head, she was dehydrated and barely breathing when, she was found,

Alone Volume 1

her shirt and bra had been cut off of her, but there wasn't any signs of sexual assault" explains Doctor Conrad.

"Where was she found Dr." asks Stan

"She was found in a field close to where one of the, cities notorious biker gangs hang out" answers Dr. Conrad

"I know which one it is, thanks doc" says Stan

"Now if you want folks, you can sit in the family room, until Lisa comes back from her x rays, I will call you, when she returns" says the doctor.

Pacing back and forth in the family waiting room, Peggy waited for Lisa to come back or the doctor to come in and tell them that she was back; Peggy looks at Kathy who was sitting there.

"I don't know how I am going to repay you for, staying with me most of the night, this is so devastating for me, she is my baby and if I lost her, I don't know what I would do" explains Peggy

"And were going to stay with you, for as long as you need Peggy" offers Kathy

"Thanks that is kind of you, I hate for Rick to miss school, because of this but it is 4:00 am, why isn't she back yet" says Peggy

The nurse finally came and said that Lisa was in her room in the ICU, Rick Katy and Peggy headed to the ICU ward with the nurse.

"I must tell you she is a lucky girl to be alive, we won't know the x ray results for a couple of hours, but you might want to know she is sleeping and heavily medicated to reduce the swelling around her wounds, you three can go see her, but you have ten minutes, Lisa needs her rest" explains the nurse.

"I understand" says Peggy, the room was in darkness and, the sound of oxygen, and heart monitor did, their job, Lisa was lying flat on her back, with tubes, down her throat, Peggy grabbed a chair and sat beside Lisa's bedside and started to sob, and pray for a sign, Rick and Katy stood back praying for Lisa's speedy recovery, the ten minute time frame had passed and the nurse came in and said.

"Okay its time, we must let her rest, why don't you go home and get some sleep and we will call when she wakes up" says the nurse.

"I have to do some stuff, and I will be back to stay with, her she needs her mother and her friends right, now" says Peggy.

"Yes but Miss. Monroe, you need to rest as well, Lisa would want you to, now at this stage were not sure what kind of condition she will be in, but what can tell you is she is going to need some serious therapy, to bounce back emotionally" replies the nurse

Heading out of the hospital Wednesday May 5th 6:00 am twelve hours after she was taken, Peggy, Kathy and Rick left to go, home feeling hungry and wanting something to eat and needing to head to her job to tell her boss what, happened, Kathy and Rick stayed by Peggy.

"I need to stop by the school after breakfast and let the school know what happened, and yes I am buying breakfast, for everyone's troubles" demands Peggy

"Good Idea, it looks as though Rick you're going to get a day off, but this is allowed right now Lisa needs to know that your, by her side.

Heading for breakfast, and doing what she had to do, the last stop was the school, Peggy parks and Kathy and Rick head inside with, her to Mrs. Jones.

"Miss Monroe" says Mrs. Jones

"What can I do for you, this morning?" asks Mrs. Jones

"Lisa won't be in school for a while, she was attack yesterday I should have picked her up at the dentist office" says Peggy

"Attacked how, I thought she went home after the dentist, most kids do, well this is a shock, and how is she doing"? Asks Mrs. Jones

"Hard to say she is in ICU at Metropolitan Hospital" replies Peggy

"Oh wow, I am so sorry, I will let Veronica know" says Mrs. Jones

"If you don't mind I will let, her know" demands Peggy

"As you wish Miss. Monroe, it is my job" replies Mrs. Jones

Rick, Peggy and Kathy walked down to room 8D, to Miss Veronica Appleton's class room, Miss Appleton was, teaching, when Peggy knocked at the door,

"Miss Monroe, Mrs. Bell and Rick, what can I do for you?" asks Miss Appleton

"Just wanted to tell you, that Lisa won't be in class for a while, she was attacked yesterday on her way back from the dentist office" explains Peggy

"Oh my okay thanks for telling me, what hospital is she in?" asks Miss Appleton, who was trying to stay strong.

"Metropolitan Hospital ICU, she's in rough shape" explains Peggy

"I will have her homework for her, and I assume when Rick is back he will bring it to her, while she is recovering" replies Miss Appleton.

After the news to Miss Appleton was delivered, Peggy headed to the apartment to get some clothes for herself and some undergarments for

Lisa, then headed back to the bells house, back at the house, Peggy and Kathy and Rick rested, things were quite, around the house, until Stan walked in

"Peggy we have got the men who did this, and I think you're to want to hear this" says Stan

"We arrest six men, thirty five year old Luke "Diesel" Lewis, thirty eight year old Scott "Gas Man Hill, and forty-nine year old Hector the Gorilla Davis" explains Stan

"Did you just say, Scott Hill?" asks Peggy in a concerned voice

"Yes I did" Miss Monroe

"That the fucking Son of a Bitch, he put his hands on my daughter" mutters Peggy

"Problem Miss Monroe" answers Stan

"Yes he is my ex-husband, we moved to get away from his crap, dam it I can't believe he did that" says Peggy.

"You didn't mention that you were having ex-husband issues Miss Monroe" says Stan

"I didn't think he would do what he did to Lisa so it didn't cross my mind at the time" says Peggy.

"Understandable, in times of great panic we tend to forget the important details, not to worry I am not going to arrest you" laughs Stan

"No, aww dam I like a pair of silver bracelets" jokes Peggy

After a few hours rest, Rick and Peggy head over to the hospital, to see how Lisa was doing and to find out her x ray results.

"Miss Monroe I see your, back just in time too, I was going to call you" says the nurse

"Really how is she?" asks Peggy

"Well she was awake, but I think you better bring her a change of underwear though she peed about 4 times and emptied her bowels, during her ordeal" says the nurse with a disgusted voice

"Poor thing, she must have been traumatized and when I get my hands on the bastard that did this, he's going to pay" mutters Peggy.

"I have a change for her, what was the result of the x ray?" asks Peggy

"I will the doctor, hold on" replies the nurse

"Miss Monroe and Mr. Bell right this way please" says the doctor

Entering into Dr. Conrad's office Rick and Peggy sit down in front of the desk

Alone Volume 1

"Miss Monroe, I have Lisa's x ray's here and, well she's got a cracked skull and sever whiplash and lots of burses" explains Dr. Conrad

"What about brain damage, is there any of that?" asks Peggy

"It's too early to tell the good sign is when she was awake she, was able to move her hands and legs but even those have ligature marks from the ropes that were used to bound her" explains Dr. Conrad.

"Can we go see, her or is that allowed" replies Peggy

"You can I will have nurse burns take you to see her" says Dr. Conrad.

Walking down the hall way to see Lisa, Peggy was fighting back the tears she followed Nurse Burns to the ICU, as she turned the corner, to go to Lisa's room Nurse Burns stops to look at Peggy and Rick and Kathy

"I must tell you that, Lisa is unresponsive and it's not good right now so you can go and see her, but only for a short time" explains Nurse Burns.

Alone Volume 1

Chapter 9
Written by Shawn Downey

Nurse Burns led Peggy and Rick to Lisa's room, when Peggy and Rick entered, Lisa was laying there still hooked up to the, machines, Rick was falling apart inside, trying to hold back his tears, the pain of seeing his girlfriend in the condition that she is in, is hard on him, Rick sat down on the other side of Peggy who was at Lisa's head touching her hand and talking to her.

"If you can hear me Lisa this is Mom, I have Rick with me we will be here when you wake up, I am terribly sorry for the ordeal you're going through I should have, been there for you" cries Peggy, Rick who was sitting beside Peggy, was wiping his eyes and the sniffle gave it away that he was starting to cry.

"Come here Rick, I know it's hard let it out" comforts Peggy

"It… just… pains… me… to see her like this… she is so full of life, and this isn't her" stutters Rick

"Yes I know, I just hope there is no damage done to her brain, I appreciate what you have done for us, but I think I am going to go home, and sleep in my own bed tonight, this has been a rough twenty four hours" says Peggy

"Well if it's okay with you, I would like to come and keep you company, I don't think you should be alone right now" suggests Rick

"You talk to your mom, and see what she says, I don't see an issue with it" says Peggy while Rick and Peggy were by Lisa's hospital bed, she made a slight movement with her hand, which caught Peggy off guard, with her mom's voice and the stroking of her hand Lisa opened her eyes

She looked at her mom and rick with an attempted smile, Rick got up and went to get nurse Della Burns, nurse burns ran with Rick to the room and she began to take out the throat tube out of Lisa's mouth, with a sick tray in front of Lisa, Della slowly takes out the tube, trying not to hit her gage reflexes, the removal was a success, the tube came out, without any issues, Nurse Burns looked at Lisa and gave her some water to moistens her throat.

"Lisa do you know where you are, at?" asks Nurse Burns

Lisa looks around, trying to focus her, eyes, she then looks straight at Rick and Mom then turns to Nurse Burns and says in a low voice.

"I am in the hospital" answers Lisa

"You are yes, you were attacked" explains Nurse Burns

"Can you move your hands at all sweetie" asks Nurse Burns

Lisa moved her fingers slowly, that brought a smile to everyone's face to see that she has, movements, then Nurse Burns asks Lisa to move her toes, Lisa cringes in pain when she does move them but she was able to move them.

"Not great for toes but I am assuming the legs are stiff" explains Nurse Burns

Next Lisa was asked to lift one leg just a little bit off the bed; Lisa also cringed in pain with that task as well.

"I think this is enough action for the day" replies Nurse Burns

Peggy and Rick got up and left the unit, heading out to the truck to go back to Ricks house, Rick has offered to stay at the apartment with Peggy until Lisa is released from the hospital, Peggy and Rick headed back to his place where his mom and dad were waiting for them to come back.

"Good you guys are back" replies Stan

"Scott will be appearing before a judge on charges of kidnapping, now they want you to testify that you, and him were having marriage problems, and if Lisa is well enough to, she is going to have as well" explains Stan

"She only just woke up, when were there and she does have some movement but its not looking good, they have removed the tubes and everything, so she is breathing on her own, not talking much" explains Peggy.

"Well that is a good sign but he goes for his hearing tomorrow, now I can take you down to the court house, if you want" says Stan

"Yeah I will go I need to face him for what he did to my little girl" says Peggy

"Now you're more than welcome to stay here, as long as you want Peggy we don't want you to be alone" says Kathy

"I was going to go back home and sleep in my own bed you have been very nice people to me, and I don't know how I am going to repay you for what you have done, but Rick has offered to stay with me if that is okay with you" explains Peggy

"That's okay I was thinking that if you go home I would get you some protection, dealing with bikers, isn't easy, they get out of jail and the retaliation can be devastating but were going to work hard to keep them off the streets the biker gang has been shut down" explains Stan

"Where is he being held at?" asks Peggy

"Rikers Island" replies Stan

Alone Volume 1

"I might head out there, to see him, I need to tell him something" says Peggy

"If it makes you feel better but don't do anything to land yourself in jail" replies Stan

"I can't guarantee that" laughs Peggy

"Rick might as well go with you then if he is going to stay with you" replies Kathy

"I will make sure he gets to school, I will drive him" offers Peggy

"That's is nice of you, keep track of your gas receipts for the, times you take him to school and pick him up, we will pay you back" says Kathy

Rick and Peggy leave to head out to Rikers Island Correctional Facility, Peggy meant business, Rick didn't say much on the drive he was just, still upset because of the condition that poor Lisa was in, once they arrived to Rikers, Peggy finds a parking spot in the visitors section and her and Rick made what seemed like a three day walk when it was only really a ten minute walk to the main entrance of the jail.

Peggy entered in through the main doors and went up to the guards desk and checked in

"Hi I am Peggy Monroe I am here to see my ex-husband Scott Hill" explains Peggy

"I will get someone to get him just go to the glass there and have a seat, you will have to talk to him with that phone there" explains the Guard.

Peggy followed the one guard that was leading her to the visitation area; Rick sat in the main lobby area, and waited for Peggy to be, done. Peggy sat down, and three guards were bring Scott to the window, Peggy filled up with rage when she saw him the guards sat Scott down took off the handcuffs and shackled his feet to the chair and stood by as he picked the phone.

"Peggy Hi" says Scott

"Don't you Peggy me you fucken fat Son of a bitch piece of shit, you put your grubby hands on my baby, and now she is in the hospital recovering for her injuries, why the hell did you do it?" asks Peggy.

"It was only just to scare her into telling me where you lived at now, I didn't want this to get out of hand, like it did, Peggy I regret what I did, the police are charging me with kidnapping and attempted murder, and attempted sex assault, you have to believe me Peggy I never meant it to get out of hand" pleads Scott

"Don't give me that crap Scott you knew full well what you were doing, and you have what's coming to you, I will make sure they lock you up, and throw away the key, and as for us were over, I am filing for divorce" yells Peggy

"You don't mean that you're angry" says Scott

"You dam rights I mean it, were through I never want to see you fat ugly face again, do you hear me and if they ever let you, out there will be mandatory restrictions in place to avoid you from coming anywhere near Lisa and myself, do I make myself clear" demands Peggy

"Yes very clear, I never thought I would come to this, I was going to change and I was working a job like you said" replies Scott

"I don't care anymore about you, it's over" repeats Peggy

Peggy hangs up the phone and goes to the main entrance where Rick is waiting, Rick follows her outside and they head to the truck, in the truck Peggy sits and tries to calm down

"Feel better that you got things off your, chest?" asks Rick

"Yes I do feel better, we can move on, now let's go to my place I need to have a shower and work tomorrow" says Peggy.

Back at Peggy and Lisa's place Rick set up an foamy that Peggy had in the living, he felt obligated to stay with Peggy while Lisa was in the hospital, Peggy had her shower then came back out in her pajama's she smiles at Rick who is sitting at the kitchen table, she looks at says.

"What would like to eat?" ask Peggy

"I am not picky whatever you are going to cook" replies Rick

"Well that's no help I am not sure what I want either" laughs Peggy

After deciding on ordering Chinese food, Rick offered to pay for the, food so that Peggy didn't have to spend any money.

"I will pay for the food when it comes, you're going to have lots of medical bills with Lisa's stay in the hospital" say Rick

"I know I am not sure how I am going to pay for them, I might have to go back to the Downtown bar that I was working at, and make more tips" says Peggy

"You will figure something out" replies Rick

"I suppose I will, I just don't like seeing her like that, she was struggling to move her legs what if she is in a wheelchair Rick, you I wonder that now, or if she is going to the same girl that I have raised" states Peggy

"Only time will tell but Lisa is strong she fight through this" replies Rick

Alone Volume 1

"I hope your right seeing her with all those tubes in her mouth was painful my little girl laying there in a hospital bed, with tubes to help her breath" cries Peggy.

After a late supper Peggy retires to bed, for the night and Rick does the same thing it has been a long day for both and after seeing Lisa, in the condition that she was in was exhausting Rick set his alarm for school, this was the first day back, for him after missing the day before he knows there's going to be questions regarding Lisa, and he would try to answer them the best that he could

The night was quite you could hear a pin drop it was so quite Rick slept soundly and so did Peggy, and at 6:00 am the alarm went off, Rick got up and went to the bathroom and cleaned up a bit, Peggy got up and was getting breakfast.

"Morning Rick" says Peggy

"Morning how did you sleep Peggy?" asks Rick

"Good I feel rested and ready to take on the day" answers Peggy

"There is cereal here I am not sure what kind you like but help yourself this is what Lisa and I do in the mornings" says Peggy

Rick has his breakfast, as Peggy gets her purse ready for work and her lunch, as soon as Rick was done eating, he grabbed the bagged lunch that was packed for him, and he headed out of the apartment with Peggy, to the truck, getting into the truck the school bus went passed, Peggy offered to drive Rick to school while he is staying with her, arriving at the school Peggy drop's Rick off at the doors and says

"I will be outside waiting for you, when your done school have a good day Rick" says Peggy. Rick waves goodbye and heads into the school his heart is pounding and he is sweating he knows he is going to have questions to answer and he doesn't feel comfortable doing that, Rick heads to his class room, where Miss Appleton was in the room already.

"Hi Rick your back" says Miss Appleton

"Yeah I don't want to be here I would rather be at the hospital" replies Rick

"Yeah I went down yesterday to see, her poor thing she was struggling to move her hands and feet there was movement, and her voice was very raspy" explains Veronica

"That would from the tube that they had in her throat" says Rick

"That makes sense, poor Peggy those medical bills must be, hurting her financially, there has to be away to raise some money to pay all the bills for her, why don't we sit down and plan that at lunch I will then go and talk

92

to Mrs. Jones to see if we can have a school fundraiser, to help her mom with medical expenses" suggests Miss Appleton

"You could try, Lisa tells me she is not popular at this school, I am the only one that talks to her besides you and Mrs. Jones, besides she's shy too" says Rick

"I understand but the school community should be able to, gather together and help out with the expenses" replies Miss Appleton.

"Yes we can plan this, I have a hard time keeping secrets though I am staying with Peggy right now, so that she has someone around" says Rick

"So lunch then we can come up with some ideas and start raising money" says Miss Appleton.

The class had finally arrived, once everyone was in their seats and quite Miss Appleton began to speak.

"Class before we start, I want to bring up something that has happened to one of our students in the class, Lisa Monroe the shy girl who sits in the empty desk there, has been hurt very badly, and is in the hospital, now I know some of you don't really talk to her, and it's sad because she is one of the students, so what I want to do is have a fundraiser for her, to help pay for the treatments at the hospital" explains Miss Appleton.

One of the students in the class Sarah Russel, the school president, raises her hand

"Yes Sarah" says Miss Appleton

"Lisa is such a nice person very shy and keeps to herself, I am saddened to hear that she is hurt badly and I think as your school president I think, she should raise money for Lisa, healthcare is expensive and I don't care how much money as person as it's hard to pay the medical bills" says Sarah.

"Okay I am meeting with Rick, who is Lisa's friend and we are going to plan the fundraiser" says Miss Appleton.

"Excuse me students, would Rick Bell come to the office please" announces Mrs. Jones

Rick got up and headed to Mrs. Jones office, as Miss Appleton began to teach her class

"Mr. Bell nice to see you, come have a seat" says Mrs. Jones

"We are deeply saddened to hear about Lisa and thoughts and prayers are, with her for a speedy recovery, that's not why I called down here though" says Mrs. Jones

"No why did you call me?" asks Rick

Alone Volume 1

"Well I called you to let you know that the school is going to everything in its power to raise money for Lisa I was talking to Miss Appleton and she agreed, and our school president that is in your class Sarah Russel, so I need you to keep this a secret from Peggy Monroe I know you and Lisa are very close and I know you have been probably helping her out since this started, that is all for now, we will get something going and get as much money raised as we can" replies Mrs. Jones

After Rick was done with Mrs. Jones he heads back to class on his way back he sees Peggy heading into the school, looking like she had something important to say, she spots Rick.

"Rick I just got a call from the hospital they want to talk to me, I need you I have already spoken to your mom, and it's okay to pulled out for the day again, so get your stuff and I will talk to Mrs. Jones, Rick ran back to the class room and grabbed his bag and asked Miss Appleton for the homework for the day and for Lisa's home, work Rick quickly explains why he is going to leave. Rick heads out of the class with homework assignments and went to Peggy's truck, Rick gets in and Peggy takes off heading to the hospital.

"What is wrong with Lisa?" asks Rick

"They wouldn't tell me, I was called at work to go down work knows what's going on and they have agreed to help out anyway they can" explains Peggy

They arrived at the hospital, Rick and Peggy ran in as soon as they were parked, heading to the nurses desk, where Nurse Della Burns was sitting she meets them at the desk.

"Mrs. Monroe, glad you can make it" says Nurse Burns

"What is wrong with her?" asks Peggy

"Dr. Conrad is waiting in his office for you" replies Nurse Burns

Peggy and Rick went to Dr. Conrad's office; he was sitting there doing paperwork.

"Peggy good see you, please have a seat" says Dr. Conrad

"Break it to me gently Doc, what is wrong with Lisa?" asks Peggy

"Oh nothing, in fact she has made remarkable progress, we did another scan and there is no brain damage, just a fractured skull, which will heal, now Lisa is going to have to have extensive counseling or just love and support, she woke last night screaming in terror, we had to calm her down, he gave her a relaxant to settle her down, and once she was calm she was asking for you and Rick, now I understand your at work and that you're going to have to pay the medical bills, but I have a surprise for you, the

Alone Volume 1

NYPD Precinct No. 3 has donated a large sum money now, I have instructions that you and Lisa are to keep that for yourselves and have enough to live on, you have a very girl there Mrs. Monroe, not handicapped special but special big hearted special" explains Dr. Conrad.

"I don't know what to say in regards to the money, I am going to have to thank the NYPD, and I am happy that she is doing so good, can we go see her, it was hard for me work knowing she is in the hospital.

"You don't have to say anything and before you go and see Lisa, Edward Barnwell and Associate's donated money to cover all of the medical bills, assume that is your place of work" says Dr. Conrad.

"Yes that is where I work I am so grateful for the things that people have done for us" replies Peggy

Rick and Peggy got up from Dr. Conrad's office and headed to see Lisa, they walked down the hall, and a nurse was coming out of her, room the nurse smiled as Rick and Peggy walk in to the room,

"Lisa honey" says Mom

"Mommy, I missed you" cries Lisa

"And Rick I have missed you too" replies Lisa

"How are you feeling my girl?" asks Mom

"Really good mom, look at what I can do" says Lisa

Lisa was able to fully move her legs and arms with no issue, with tears in her eyes Peggy says.

"That is awesome sweetie, I prayed that you would be able to move again" says Mom

"And the nurse said if I can walk tommrow down the hall, then I can go home" says Lisa

"That is so cool honey, you have one hell of a boyfriend here, Lisa he and his family have been so kind" says Mom

"I told you, he was good people" replies Lisa

"But if they're going to get me up walking I need to put on some underwear I am freezing" giggles Lisa

"I brought some down for you plus a bra I will have to bring a change of clothes down for you when you are ready to come home" says Mom.

"Yeah they washed my other pants and stuff and put them in my locker and the shirt that I had on, but that is torn, where are my glasses?" asks Lisa

"I have them in my purse, honey here you go" says Mom

Alone Volume 1

"So Miss Appleton was in yesterday, she cried when she saw me, I guess I was in bad shape" says Lisa

"Yes you were, they didn't know what was wrong with you or if you would be the same again or if you would ever walk again, but the moving around is a start" says Mom

"Yeah but I would love to get up to use the washroom instead of using a bed pan" says Lisa

"Speaking of which I have to use the pan" replies Lisa

"I will get the nurse then Lisa" says Mom

"No you don't have too, I am using it pretty good I just need her to empty it, when I am done" replies Lisa

"Well I will give you the bed pan and we will close the curtain and let you do what you have to do in peace, I am sure you don't want me looking at you or Rick looking there" laughs Mom

"You changed my diapers you know what I have, and as for Rick he will see it eventually" giggles Lisa.

Mom handed her the bed pan closed the curtain and let Lisa do what she had to do, Rick went to get the nurse, as soon as Lisa said she was done, nurse burns comes in and takes the bed pan and empties it, back talking to her mom Lisa covers her legs up with the blanket.

"I am going to go to the cafeteria for a coffee, do you want anything Rick" offers Peggy

"A coke please" answers Rick

"I could really use a coke to mom" says Lisa

"No I am not going to do that, when you get out you can have one" replies mom

Peggy got up went down the hall to the cafeteria, this gave Lisa and Rick a chance to talk

"Thanks for being here for me and my mom Rick, I can't thank everyone enough for being so kind" says Lisa

"No Problem I love you that's why I am being nice" says Rick

"I love you too Rick" replies Lisa

Peggy came back with, a coffee for herself a coke for Rick and an apple juice for, Lisa sitting and visiting Lisa is grateful to be alive.

Alone Volume 1

Chapter 10

Written by Shawn Downey

The Visit with Lisa had to be cut short, when nurse burns came in and says.

"It's time for Lisa's bath, if you want to stay longer you can, I am just going to bath her, and going to see if she can walk to the tub" says Nurse Burns

"So if I walk to the tub and back, does that mean I can get out of here and get back to life?" asks Lisa

"If you can and you have a good night, then in the morning I will get Dr. Conrad to release you and you can go home" says Nurse Burns

Nurse Burns had a house coat in her hand and she hands it to Lisa as she closes the curtain she says"

"Take off the gown and put the house coat on and we will walk to the tub, I will grab some underwear from your mom too when we come back" says Nurse Burns

The curtain opened and Peggy and Rick watched as Nurse Burns helps Lisa off the bed, sitting on the edge of her, hospital bed, Lisa lets her feet dangle as they dangled; Nurse Burns went across the hall, to run the water in the bath tub.

"How are you feeling with your legs dangling darling?" asks Mom

"Good, I am ready to do this, I am ready to walk to the tub and have my bath, and walk back" say Lisa

"You will do fine, you have done good up to this point, so I have faith in you that you can do this" says mom.

Nurse Burns comes back and stands in the room about feet from the side of the bed where Lisa is sitting.

"Okay you can get up, I will have my arms out to help you if you should stumble" says Nurse Burns

Lisa always eager to do stuff puts her hands on the bed and pushes herself off the bed with her feet hitting the floor, she is standing, getting the blood flow to her legs Lisa takes the first step, a little off balance she walks the two feet, to nurse burns and the two go off to the bath tub that is waiting with hot water and the jets going.

"This bath will loosen up your muscles they have been still, and they need to limber up so that you can walk out of here tomorrow with a clean bill of health" says Nurse Burns

"That will be nice, I am grateful for the help that I have been getting here, I am going to miss you when I go home" replies Lisa

Alone Volume 1

"I am going to miss you too young lady, you're a sweetheart" compliments Nurse Burns.

Lisa took off the house coat and she climbed the steps to the tub, getting in Lisa can already feel the water on her feet she slowly sits down

"Oh this feels so good, its nice to have a real bath, I feel so dirty" says Lisa

"Well when you came in you weren't in the best of shape we did have to sponge bath you" says Nurse Burns

"Why?" asks Lisa

"When you were found, you had peed and pooped your pants about four times" says Nurse Burns.

"Oh okay, I was pretty scared, I am fourteen I shouldn't have done that, I am not two years old or in diapers" says Lisa

"Sweetie it happens you, weren't in good shape, when you came in we didn't know what condition you were in, you were bleeding from your head" explains Nurse Burns

"Is that why my hair feels gross" says Lisa

"Yes that would be that is why I am going to give you a hair wash, the night of pampering is over, I think you have done well, so far Lisa" replies Nurse Burns

Lisa slides down into the tub more, as Nurse Burns runs water down through her hair, and applies the shampoo and srubs Lisa's head, the whole bath took about thirty minutes to complete, when Lisa was done, she walks back to her room without nurse burns, her mom and Rick were waiting for her, Nurse Burns came back into the room smiling.

"Eager Beaver isn't she, I looked up and she was gone" says Nurse Burns

"That's my Lisa" laughs mom

As Lisa sits back on the bed nurse burns got the clean pair of underwear out and Lisa puts them on, with the curtain closed.

"We will close the curtain again, I don't think your brother wants to see you naked" says Nurse Burns

"He's not my brother, he is my boyfriend" says Lisa

"Oh well that's good, I am happy for you" replies Nurse Burns

Once Lisa had on her underwear, she swings her legs on to the bed and the curtain opens.

"I am going to leave you three alone for now, but if you need anything Lisa I will be on tonight" says Nurse Burns.

"Mom did you bring a brush?" asks Lisa

Alone Volume 1

"Yes I did honey" replies Mom

Peggy got up and sat on the edge of the bed, and started to brush Lisa's hair, Lisa looks at Rick with a smile and says to him.

"You can come closer to me, I don't bite, you haven't said much of anything" says Lisa

"I didn't like seeing you in the shape you were in Lisa, I have been very worried about you, now that you're doing good and possibly getting out tomorrow, I can start feeling better knowing that I am going to have my girl back" explains Rick

Rick moved closer as Peggy brushes, Lisa's hair once it was all brushed out, Peggy looks at her watch.

"Oh it's getting late" replies Peggy, just then a voice comes over the intercom.

"Attention all visitors, visiting hours are now over, please say your goodbyes and come back at regular visiting hours, thanks for visiting Metropolitan Hospital" says the voice

"Okay if you're to go, I am going to go to sleep that bath relaxed me" says Lisa

Putting the blanket over Lisa, Peggy gives Lisa a big hug and kiss, and then Lisa looks over at Rick and says.

"Come here" says Lisa

Rick goes over to Lisa's bed side and looks at her pretty blue, eyes Lisa reaches up and gives Rick a big kiss on the lips then she opened her arms for a hug, Rick hugged and Lisa says

"I love you Rick thanks for being here" says Lisa

"I love you too Lisa, I will be here for you" replies Rick

Peggy and Rick said their good nights and headed out of Lisa's room and down the hall to the main doors, with light rain outside and going on 8:30pm Rick and Peggy head back to the truck, getting into the truck, Peggy looks at Rick who seems more relaxed and says"

"What would you like to eat, I know it's late, let's just grab some McDonalds or something suggests Peggy

"McDonalds is fine, I am too hungry to wait for food" laughs Rick.

After grabbing a bite to eat and heading to the apartment, Rick and Peggy relaxed for the rest of the night it had been a long day, and knowing that Lisa has made progress in her recovery, after about an hour of sitting up and relaxing Peggy decides to go to bed and sleep, she said goodnight to Rick and went to her room, sleeping in the living room. Rick set his alarm and went to sleep, he could hear the rain falling, the smell of the rain coming in through the window of the apartment, made it easy for sleeping.

At 6:00 am the alarm went off, Rick got up and went to the bathroom then got dressed and ready for school, Peggy was just getting ready for her day as well, she thought about Lisa and how she faired last night, Peggy knew Lisa was in good hands at the hospital and when she was ready to come home they would call but deep down inside Peggy knew that Lisa would have difficulty coping with this and she would need the love and support and her and Rick could do that, then she thought a lot about Scott and why he did what he did, she was over him now but it is what he did that made her mad, she can't worry about him she's got Lisa to worry about once she is out of the hospital.

"You're in deep thought this morning" says Rick

"Just thinking about Lisa I wish she was home seeing the empty bedroom is hard" says Peggy.

"Until she is comes home I will stay here with you, I love Lisa to much not to stay with her mom during this time of need" replies Rick

"That is so sweet of you, Rick Lisa loves you too and you know I am starting to love you too I am starting to realize that you are the kind of boy my daughter needs you have brought her out of her shell, I was always wondering if she would come out of her shell, now this set back is going to put her back there, and sabotage the progress that we have already made" says Peggy

"That is what I was afraid of too, but I think we can work with her as long as we are there for her when she needs us" says Rick.

Rick and Peggy headed downstairs to the truck, Peggy was going to take Rick to school and then go to work, in the truck and on the way to school dealing with the morning traffic, Rick looks at his watch, not worrying if he was going to late he knows that he won't be, they finally got to the school and Rick gets out and heads into the school, getting books from his locker the school president came to his locker.

"Well since you weren't in class yesterday to help out with a fundraiser for your girlfriend, we couldn't come up with anything" snarls Ashely

"Is it my fault that I was pulled out of class no it's not my fault and its fine anyway there has been people that have come through for Lisa and her mom" explains Rick

Alone Volume 1

"I am not sure what you see in her, I mean she just sits and doesn't say a word I mean it must be a pretty boring conversation if she doesn't say anything" says Ashely

"For your information she talks a lot to me and she is coming out of her shell, she is just shy that's all" explains Rick

"I think you can do better than her don't you want some girl that is more intelligent than her" laughs Ashely

"If you're talking about yourself Ashely I am not interested in you, for some reason you think that I am but I am not, we have been in the same school for two and half years now and I have had no interest in you, you're a snob and you get what you want when you throw a tantrum just because your mother sits on the PTA, for your info I love Lisa Monroe" says Rick

"Rick Bell all the gull to say that to me, do you have any idea of the power that my mother has on the PTA, if she finds out that you spoke to me, like that you will be suspended" replies Ashely

"Bite me Baker your mother can't do crap to me" snarls Rick

"Bite you, no I will get your girlfriend to do that, if you want to hang around with trash then you can, and I hope your unhappy in your relationship" says Ashely

Rick walked into class and took his seat Ashely was sitting in her usual spot in front of the class middle row, like the goody two shoes that she is, Miss Appleton walks in and sits at her desk, the rest of the class comes in and Miss Appleton gets started teaching, the morning was just catch-up for Rick he had missed a couple of days, do to Lisa's ordeal, The first four hours of class Rick had issues concentrating, seeing the empty desk beside him, the lunch bell rang and the students left for lunch Rick was getting up to head to the cafeteria when Miss Appleton stopped him.

"You seem distracted today Rick, I am worried about you the homework that has been assigned to you hasn't been getting done lately it's not like you to not do this" says Miss Appleton

"I appreciate your concern but I am fine I have the work done I was just going over it before I hand it in, at the end of the day" replies Rick

"I gave everyone a catch-up time I expected the work to be handed in Rick before lunch, now you can go for lunch but I want that attitude to change this isn't the Rick I know" says Miss Appleton.

Rick heads to the cafeteria and gets his lunch he decided not to sit in the cafeteria, he went and sat in the court yard of the school, the first time he and Lisa sat there, on their first lunch together, Rick thought a lot about what Miss Appleton said and he realized he hasn't been the same person, he has strong feelings for Lisa and he has been very concerned, then he thought about Ashely and the way he spoke to her, Rick got up and headed back inside to the cafeteria Ashely was sitting with her click, Ashely looks up at Rick with a disgusted look on her face and says to him

"What do you want" snarls Ashely

"We need to talk" replies Rick

Heading out to talk Rick knows what he is going to say to Ashely is going to apologize for saying what he said to her.

"Ashely I am sorry for saying what I did to you okay I have been under a lot of pressure I love Lisa and it won't change the feelings that I have for her and if you don't like it that's too bad" says Rick

"I accept your apology and if you love Lisa then I can accept that I always thought though that we had something you and I" says Ashely

"What we had in elementary is different were in junior high, I seen something in Lisa she's a good looking girl and she's cute, and your cute Ashely, but our lives are so different, if something should happen that Lisa and I don't work out I might consider asking you out but, what we have right now is special and with her in the hospital its hard on me" explains Rick

"I understand now Rick" answers Ashely

The bell rang to end lunch Rick headed back to class, and took his seat, the afternoon class with Miss Appleton was math class, Rick got out his appropriate books and he waited for Miss Appleton to arrive, Miss Appleton, comes into the class and closes the door, then on her desk she puts down a stack of papers.

"Text books closed class, we are having a math quiz" says Miss Appleton

Rick was shocked for the fact that there was a surprise quiz, Miss Appleton handed everything out and gave the class thirty minutes to complete the quiz, Rick looks at the quiz and smiles to himself as he thought *This one will be easy I was just doing these equations thinks Rick.*

Rick and the rest of the class completed the quiz in the time that Miss Appleton gave, then she got the class to work on the novel for English until the bell for the end of the day, Rick had all his homework ready and he gets up and puts it on Miss Appleton' desk then sits back down, Rick looks over at the clock as the time seems to be going slow

The 3:15 bell finally rang to signal the end of the day and the end of the school week, Rick grabs his books and his bag and heads out the doors to the waiting truck, Rick gets into the truck and Peggy greets him with a smile as they drive off.

"I have some good news for you" says Peggy

"What's the good news?" asks Rick

"Lisa gets to come home today" says Peggy

"That is fantastic news, she should be happy to come she will have the weekend to rest and then back to school on Monday" says Rick

"Yes that is the plan, to have her back at the school" says Peggy

Arriving at the Metropolitan Hospital and parking, Peggy and Rick head into the hospital to the nurses station to the waiting nurse burns.

"Glad you guys are here Lisa has made a full recovery and she has been itching all day for you and Rick to come" says Nurse Burns

"That is fantastic" cries Peggy

"Signing the discharge papers Nurse Burns sends another nurse to go and get Lisa, Rick is feeling anxious to see Lisa walk out, he heard her talking to the nurse he couldn't see her but then he saw her head, the nurse had brought her in a wheel chair, Lisa stands up when she sees her mom and Rick and she gave them both big hugs.

"I am ready mom" says Lisa

"Before you go, you will need to see the doctor in two weeks for a check-up" replies Nurse Burns, Lisa shook her head in agreement that she would see Dr. Conrad, heading out to the truck Lisa Peggy and Rick, headed for the apartment before that happened Peggy asked Rick.

"Did you want to go home or stay one more night at our place?" asks Peggy

"I will stay one more night at your place then I will go home now that Lisa is home I want you two to spend some time together" replies Rick.

"Your part of this family too Rick I mean you have done so much for us so far I feel like Lisa and I owe you a great deal of gratitude for your kindness" says Peggy

"I am doing this out of the goodness of my heart I love Lisa and this is the least I can do for her" replies Rick

Heading home Lisa was looking around and just happy to be in the company of her mother and her boyfriend when they got to the apartment Peggy parked and they walked in looking at the stairs Lisa kind of hesitated on climbing the steps Lisa took it one step at a time slowly walking up to the second floor, once arriving at the apartment door Lisa was excited to get inside the suit which has seem like forever since she was home.

"I am happy to be home" says Lisa

Alone Volume 1

"I'll bet you are happy to be home, now you sit down and rest Lisa I will get supper" orders Mom

"I want to help I don't need to rest mom I have been resting for a week now I need to move around" replies Lisa

"Don't argue with me Lisa, I almost lost you I want you to sit on the couch and relax I will cook us supper" repeats mom

Lisa listened to her mom's orders she sat on the couch watching TV while Rick did her job of setting the table, getting up to stretch Lisa headed to the bathroom, and then headed to her bedroom to put her folded clothes away, coming back to the living room Lisa goes to the fridge and looks for a can of coke of some juice, Lisa grabs the juice jug and pours a glass of juice then sits back down before she could sit down mom told her that supper was ready, heading to the table with her juice Lisa sits down in her chair that she sits at for suppers.

"It is nice to have a home cooked meal, that hospital food I tell you some days I could have pasted wallpaper on the wall with it says Lisa

"Yeah the foods not the greatest in the hospital" replies Mom

Lisa ate a good supper more then what she usually eats; mom looks at Lisa and says

"You must have wanted the home cooking but I see you have lost weight from being in the hospital, your smaller then what you were I am not saying your fat, but I could really see your ribs" says mom

"You know I don't put on weight I like my figure" says Lisa

"Yes you have my figure but you lost what weight you had and for someone your age and height that is not good" replies mom

"I know mom" says Lisa

After supper Lisa and Rick sat on the couch and mom sat in her chair doing a puzzle book, not feeling the greatest after eating what she did Lisa got up and headed to the bathroom, Lisa closed the door and turned on the water so that no one wouldn't hear her throwing up, Lisa threw up her supper that she ate and her lunch, thinking to herself *'I guess I shouldn't have eaten that much just getting out of the hospital thinks Lisa*, Lisa came back out of the bathroom and went to her bedroom she reached into her drawer that contains her pajama's and she put on a night shirt with no underwear and her house coat and slippers and came back to the living and joined Rick and her mother in the living room watching TV and talking until it was time for bed Lisa was looking forward to sleeping in her own room and in her own bed, the hospital wasn't a good place to sleep Lisa headed to the bathroom to brush her teeth and combed her hair, once she was done Rick did what he had to do then Lisa got to her room and then asked Rick to come to her door

"Thank you for doing this I appreciate the kindness and I am not sure how to repay you" says Lisa

"I am just happy to be your boyfriend and happy to help you out" replies Rick

"Come closer to me please" says Lisa.

Rick came closer to Lisa, Lisa grabbed his head closed the door and pushed him up against the door and kissed him on the lips, surprised by what Lisa did he smiled and left her room back to the living room too his bed

Rick lays down on the floor, still happy from the huge kiss that Lisa gave him, in the morning when Peggy Rick and Lisa were up having breakfast; Lisa was sticking by Rick like glue until they dropped him off at his house.

After that Lisa and her mom made the forty five minute trip to Trenton New Jersey to grandma, Lisa wasn't expecting that, but she went with it anyway, they pulled up to the town house that her grandmother was in

"Okay lets go I need to see Grandma Lisa" says Mom

Climbing the stairs to the town house and ringing the doorbell Peggy heard the voice heading to the door, when the door opened it was Hank.

"Hi Hank is mom home?" asks Peggy

"No I don't know where the hell she is, she left an hour ago, you could find her spending money at the bingo hall" growls Hank

"Okay I will just sit in the truck and wait for her" says Peggy

Lisa and her mom waited for grandma to come back as soon as the car pulled up Peggy and Lisa got out.

"Mom hi" says Peggy

"Peggy what the hell are you doing here you didn't tell me you were coming" replies Brenda

"I wanted to surprise you mom I haven't seen you for a while and I wanted to have a visit" says Peggy.

"Okay come in then I don't have long I have to go to work and make the money" says grandma.

"I won't be long I just want to tell you what has happened" says Peggy

"Oh what's that?" asks Brenda

"Scott is in jail charged for kidnapping and attempted murder, were done I don't love him anymore I am just happy to have Lisa back she was the one that he grabbed and I almost lost her mom" says Peggy

"He was no good for you anyway I don't know what you seen in him I am glad that Lisa here is okay and how are you doing through all this?" asks Brenda

"I am coping Mom" says Peggy

After a short visit Lisa and her mom left the town house complex where her mom lived she decided to go and see her sister Ruby with the last known address that she has for her Peggy pulled up to another town house complex and rang the doorbell, when the door opened a lady stood there

"Ruby" says Peggy

"Peggy what are you doing here it's not a good time I am just in the middle of something what brought you here?" asks Ruby

"I just wanted to see my sister who doesn't talk to me very much" says Peggy

"Well I am here god dam it now speak" snaps Ruby

"You know what I don't have to deal with this your high again aren't you still on coke right, you're never going to change Ruby" says Peggy.

"Peggy wait" yells Ruby

"What do you want this time Ruby" says Peggy

"I am in need of some help, Peggy I have relapsed again and I am not sure if I will ever come out of this, if I don't get the help that I need" cries Ruby

"You have to help yourself Ruby, no one can do it for you, not mom, not hank, not me you are the one that has to do it" replies Peggy

"Okay I will try and do the right thing" responds Ruby

"I know you can I have to worry about Lisa and myself I can't help you out" says Peggy

Peggy and Lisa get into the truck and speed off away from the neighbourhood that Ruby lives in Peggy decided to make one more stop and that was at her brother Marks place, when Peggy stopped in front of Marks House, he was sitting on the front porch.

"Oh my god is that you Peggy" says Mark

"It is me" smiles Peggy

"And Lisa you have grown to be a lovely young lady" responds mark

Peggy' brother is the only one that stayed on the straight and narrow path and Peggy too occasionally having a beer or two once in a while.

"Come in Peggy would you like anything to drink?" asks Mark

"We can't stay long just wanted to say hi and check up on everyone" says Peggy

"That's nice I am doing well and the family is everyone is out doing their thing I stayed home" replies Mark

Mark Peggy and Lisa chatted for about a half an hour then, getting into the truck and heading home back to the apartment.

THE END

You have reached the end of this first Volume stay tuned for the next one soon to come

Made in the USA
Columbia, SC
21 April 2017